T0413533

THE TRUE STORY OF A JEWISH GIRL WHO JOINED THE PARTISANS IN WORLD WAR II

FIGHTER IN THE WOODS

ALSO BY JOSHUA M. GREENE

The Girl Who Fought Back: Vladka Meed and the Warsaw Ghetto Uprising

Signs of Survival

Cowritten with Renee Hartman

My Survival: A Girl on Schindler's List

Cowritten with Rena Finder

THE TRUE STORY OF A JEWISH GIRL WHO JOINED THE PARTISANS IN WORLD WAR II

FIGHTER IN THE WOODS

JOSHUA M. GREENE

SCHOLASTIC FOCUS
New York

Library of Congress Cataloging-in-Publication Data available

ISBN 978-1-5461-3585-2

10 9 8 7 6 5 4 3 2 1 25 26 27 28 29

Printed in Italy 183

First edition, February 2025

Book design by Maithili Joshi

TO THE 1.5 MILLION CHILDREN WHO PERISHED IN THE HOLOCAUST

Prologue

EXPOSED

On a warm night in August 1943, while the rest of Poland slept, a teenager named Celia Cimmer climbed onto a stocky horse with a long, shaggy mane. She cinched the strap of her rifle across her chest and tightened her grip on the reins, preparing for a tough ride.

Celia was part of a team of thirty—twenty-eight young men and one other teenage girl—riding horses. These young people, who had all escaped from the Nazis, were partisans, a secret group that fought back from hiding places in woods and dense forests.

A scout had told the partisans that Nazi soldiers were storing a pile of ammunition in a schoolyard several miles to the east. The partisans' mission tonight was to destroy it.

Celia and her comrades quietly walked their horses through stands of trees and thick underbrush. When the schoolyard was in sight, they brought their horses to a stop. In the middle of the yard, silhouetted against the starlit sky, were boxes of dynamite, barrels of gunpowder, cans of gasoline, belts of bullets, and other weapons stacked up in a tall pile. At the far end of the yard stood an abandoned schoolhouse. Celia could hear German voices coming from inside—men talking and laughing.

The partisans didn't have much time to do their job.

Silently, the team crept into the concrete yard and pulled their horses up in front of the pile of weapons. Celia and the other teenage girl stood guard with their rifles pointed toward the schoolhouse. Several of the partisans jumped off their horses, lit gasoline-soaked rags, and threw them onto the pile of weapons. The young men jumped back on their horses and rode out of the yard at a gallop. Celia and the other girl followed close behind.

Seconds later, the pile of ammunition exploded with a deafening *Boom!* It was a roaring, earsplitting explosion, as though a bolt of lightning had hit the schoolyard. The air stung with the smell of burning gasoline, and bullets popped in the stockpile like strings of firecrackers.

Celia's horse was nearest to the explosion, and he flinched at the sound. The horse reared up on his hind legs, Celia's rifle got tangled in the reins, and she fell to the ground. Her horse galloped off.

Celia turned to see Nazi soldiers running out of the schoolhouse, yelling at the partisans and firing their weapons. Two of the soldiers lit flares and tossed them forward. The schoolyard burst into light. Celia was lying on the ground, exposed and alone. No rifle. No horse.

The soldiers took aim.

Chapter 1

WHAT THE WAR WAS REALLY ABOUT

Growing up, Celia never thought about carrying a rifle or blowing up piles of Nazi weapons.

She lived with her parents and siblings in a small town called Szarkowszczyzna (pronounced "sharkoff-schizna") in what was then eastern Poland. Today, it is a separate country called Belarus. Celia loved reading books, climbing trees with her friends, and in the summer, swimming in the clear warm water of the river that ran by her town. She was studious and took homework seriously. She dreamed of one day becoming a doctor or a lawyer.

When she was old enough to begin high school, Celia was accepted to a respected boarding school in the nearby town of Druya. She was excited to attend.

It was in Druya, on the night of June 22, 1941, that Celia's life changed forever.

She was asleep in her dormitory when the buzz of planes filled the night sky. Within minutes, bombs began falling on the town. The explosions shook Celia's dormitory like an earthquake. She awoke with a start. School officials ran through the dormitory, flinging open the doors to students' rooms.

"War has broken out!" they shouted. "The Germans are bombing. You must evacuate the building."

Two years earlier, in 1939, two nations, Nazi Germany and the Soviet Union, had divided Poland between them; Germany took over the western part of the country, while the Soviets occupied the eastern part, where Celia lived.

Now the Nazis had turned on the Soviets and were storming through eastern Poland. The air attack was preparing the way for tens of thousands of German soldiers who would soon be arriving on foot from the west.

Celia didn't even waste time changing out of her nightgown. She raced out of her room and joined other students running down the stairs and into the street. Outside, the town was in chaos. Bombs fell every few minutes with a deadly cadence—*Boom! Boom! Boom!*—and Celia covered her ears. Her only thought was to get home, but home was forty miles south. That meant running straight into the hands of the Germans.

Everyone else was running east, toward Soviet Russia. The roads leading away from Druya were jammed with Polish civilians and Soviet soldiers, terrified of being caught by the Nazis.

Celia had no idea where she could hide. Then she remembered. One of her best friends from school, a Polish Christian girl, lived nearby. Celia was sure her friend would take her in, lend her some clothes, and let Celia stay with her family for a while.

Celia ran through a maze of streets, trusting her sharp memory to steer her in the right direction. Finally, she arrived at the gate to her friend's house. Celia caught her breath and called out her friend's name.

The front door opened. Celia's friend stepped outside and walked toward the gate. Celia felt instantly better. Her friend arrived at the gate—and did nothing. She didn't open the gate or invite Celia in. She just stared at Celia as though she didn't recognize her.

Celia was confused. Her friend could see her standing there in her nightgown. She knew there were bombs falling. Why was she not inviting Celia in? Just yesterday, they'd helped each other with their homework. They'd shared secrets. Weren't they still friends?

The Polish Christian girl finally spoke.

"Get away from here, you dirty Jew!" she yelled. Then she turned, stormed back into her house, and slammed the door.

Celia stared at the closed door. She'd never felt so hurt or betrayed in her life. How could her friend have changed so quickly? Or maybe she hadn't changed. Maybe she had always felt this way about Jews but had been hiding it until now.

Celia suddenly felt foolish for having trusted their friendship. It was clear that her so-called friend was quite prepared to let Celia die in the street—because she was Jewish.

"That," Celia commented years later, "was when I understood what the war was really about."

She turned away from her former friend's house and started walking. The bombs continued to fall, destroying streets, uprooting trees, and setting fire to houses. Celia knew that, not far away, the Nazi army was approaching. But she had no choice.

She headed south, toward home—and the Nazis.

WORLD WAR II AND POLAND

World War II, also called the Second World War, was a global conflict that lasted from 1939 to 1945. Most countries of the world took part, fighting in two opposing forces: the Allies (primarily the United States, Great Britain, the Soviet Union, and France) versus the Axis powers (Nazi Germany, Fascist Italy, and Imperial Japan). The war was the result of aggressive and illegal actions taken by Germany's tyrannical leader, Adolf Hitler, to conquer Europe. Hitler intended to murder Europe's Jewish population, along with other minorities. In his fanatical racist judgment, Jews in particular were less than human and had to be eliminated.

In 1939, Hitler decided to take over Poland. To be sure that the Soviet Union would not interfere, Hitler convinced Soviet leaders to divide Poland. The western part of the country would go to Germany and the eastern part to the Soviets.

On September 1, 1939, Germany's invasion of Poland began. In response, Great Britain and France declared war on

Germany, and World War II officially started. As agreed, two weeks later, Soviet forces entered Poland from the east. Then Hitler betrayed his agreement with the Soviet Union, and in June 1941 Nazi troops occupied the portion of Poland that had been controlled by the Soviets. Nazi planes preceded Germany's ground forces, bombing towns such as Druya, where Celia was in school.

By mid-July of 1941, Nazi Germany had occupied all of Poland.

Chapter 2

MEMORIES OF HOME

Celia kept away from main roads, where the moonlight was bright and she was more likely to be seen. She walked in the shadows of wooded side roads, even though branches and rocks slowed her down. She looked left and right, kept low, ran from tree to tree, listening for the drone of planes, the stomp of soldiers' boots, or the roar of a jeep or tank. The night wind was cold. She wrapped her arms tightly around her body as she walked.

To distract herself, she thought about home.

Szarkowszczyzna was a small place, with a population of about fifteen hundred. Two out of three residents were Jewish. The town was located about four hundred miles east of Germany and one hundred miles west of Russia. From either side, an army could reach Celia's hometown in just a few days.

Szarkowszczyzna wasn't a fancy city like New York or Paris, but it had a gently flowing river and beautiful countryside. Celia loved to walk through the meadow near her home, among larkspur and bluebells so bright it seemed the flowers had fallen from the sky. There were also buttercups and dandelions, purple thistles and yellow daisies. Celia loved the mountain ash trees with their slim trunks and upward-curving branches. Mountain ash bore juicy, soft clusters of berries that were a feast for birds.

Celia's stomach growled. She hadn't eaten since yesterday. She remembered how, every summer, her mother boiled ripe elderberries in a pot over a wood-stoked fire, added sugar, and made thick jams and jellies. In autumn, vines hanging from wooden trellises in the town's fields yielded bunches of ripe red grapes. Celia remembered with a chuckle how she and her youngest sister, Slava, enjoyed kicking off their shoes and socks, cleaning their feet, and climbing into big wooden tubs to stomp on the grapes. The grapes squished between their toes, and the sweet juice flowed into oakwood vats, where it sat for months, fermenting into wine.

Celia felt a pang of sadness. She missed her siblings. She had two older sisters named Dina and Miriam, two younger sisters named Chaya and Slava, and two older brothers named Hershke and Zalman. The Cimmers were a warm, loving family. Celia's father, Shmuel, was well respected by the Jewish community of their town. He was an educated businessman whose factory manufactured flax, a fiber used in clothing, bedsheets, and tablecloths.

The family lived in a big house right on the bustling market square, and Celia's mother, Liba, ran a restaurant out of their living room. The restaurant was a popular spot for weddings and other celebrations. Celia's stomach growled again as she thought of the wonderful dishes her mother cooked so well, like fried potato dumplings and soup thick with mushrooms that grew in the nearby woods. Liba also made delicious salads from shredded carrots and beets flavored with lemon and sugar. Everyone loved her desserts, especially her poppy seed pastries and blueberry cheesecake. In the middle of the restaurant was a big silver samovar urn, where patrons could get hot water for their cups of tea.

Celia's mother was known for her kindness and generosity. Every Friday, she packed the family's wooden wagon with freshly baked loaves of bread and bottles of milk still warm from the family's cow. Then she set out with Celia and Slava to deliver groceries to needy members of the community.

Celia walked on, glancing up every few seconds to be sure she wasn't walking into the arms of Nazi soldiers. The bombing had stopped. The only sounds were night animals. A wolf howled in the distance. An owl hooted from a branch overhead.

Clouds slid in and covered the moon, and the sky turned pitch-black. Using the little light thrown off by the stars, Celia continued toward home.

To distract herself from the cold night air, Celia imagined it was a warm summer day and she was walking through the market square outside her house. On Wednesdays, farmers set out baskets of corn, barley, oats, potatoes, eggs, butter, cheese, and other foods on long wooden tables. Hundreds of customers from surrounding villages arrived in horse-drawn wagons to do their weekly shopping. There was a bakery where people lined up to buy loaves of dark bread and hot cinnamon buns. On Fridays, Jewish customers bought fresh-baked, braided challah loaves for their Shabbat meals. Celia could recall the delicious smell of that challah right now.

In the market square there was a butcher shop, a tailor, a barber, a hardware store, a doctor's office, and a blacksmith who forged shoes for horses and made repairs on wagons and furniture. A village clown wandered through the market, entertaining children while their parents shopped.

Celia knew that her hometown was a little behind the times. Hardly anybody had an indoor toilet or a sink with running water, and the dirt roads in and out of town were all unpaved. After heavy rains, the roads turned to mud, and traveling by horse and cart became impossible. When that happened, the townspeople found themselves cut off from the outside world, but nobody minded. On rainy days, the adults invited friends over for card games, and Celia and her friends played hide-and-seek. It wasn't difficult to stay busy indoors.

Recently, electric lines had been laid in Celia's part of Poland. For the first time, light bulbs hung in each room of the Cimmers' big house. Once a month, Celia's father plugged in a projector and showed movies on a white sheet tacked to the living room wall. Celia remembered how popular those Sunday movies were. Friends and neighbors filled the living room to capacity.

Celia tried not to think about the Jew-haters in her town, the boys who yelled at her, "Hey, Jew! Go to Palestine!", which was the name for Israel in those days. Instead, she thought about how much she loved her family. When cousins and aunts and uncles visited for holiday meals, the number of family members seated in the dining room often reached fifty or more. Jewish people had lived in Poland for more than a thousand years, and like Jews everywhere in the world, they observed traditional holidays, such as Hanukkah, Purim, and Passover. Celia especially liked Passover Seders, when the family took turns reading aloud the biblical story of the Exodus. Passover celebrated the time when God brought the Jews out of slavery in Egypt and Moses led them through the desert to the Promised Land.

Despite these warm memories, Celia was still shivering. She could no longer feel her toes or the tips of her fingers. She calculated that she'd gone only a few miles. At this pace, it would take days to reach home.

A truck crested the top of a hill. Celia quickly ducked behind a tree. The driver glided to a stop not far from where she was hiding and called out, "Where are you going?"

Celia had no choice but to come out and answer. Clearly, the driver had seen her.

"I'm trying to get home. Szarkowszczyzna," she said.

The driver waved her over. He lifted an overcoat from the passenger seat and handed it to her. "Put this on. Climb in the back—but stay down and keep quiet."

She'd lucked out. Someone friendly. She climbed in the back, the truck moved on, and Celia's thoughts returned to her family. She thought again about her father. When Shmuel wasn't at his flax factory, he liked to sit by the living room fireplace and read books. Celia's mother preferred to hitch up her dress, tie a kerchief over her head, and head out on a bicycle ride in the fresh air and sunshine. In those days, women who rode bicycles unescorted were considered very daring.

Daring, Celia thought as the truck continued down the bumpy road. *Here I am, daring to travel home on my own through Nazi-occupied Poland. Maybe I am more like my mother than I realized.*

The truck arrived at the outskirts of her town. They had driven most of the night, and the sky had transformed from dark blue to the pale gray of morning. Celia climbed out of the truck, thanked the driver, handed him back his coat, and walked on, relieved to be home at last.

ANTISEMITISM

Hostility or violence toward people because they are Jewish is called antisemitism or Jew-hatred. It may take the form of propaganda that declares Jewish people to be inferior, or political efforts to isolate, oppress, or otherwise injure them. Antisemitism also includes promoting prejudiced or stereotyped attitudes about Jews.

Jews are not defined only by their religious faith. They are a culture and a civilization that has thrived for thousands of years. The Jewish people originated in the Middle East, in the ancient Land of Israel. Their homeland was repeatedly conquered by other nations, and around the first century CE, the Roman Empire exiled most of the Jews to different parts of the world. This exile is known as the Diaspora. Wherever they were, Jews maintained their distinctive customs, practices, and religious beliefs.

When Adolf Hitler became chancellor of Germany in 1933, he promoted the lie that Germans were a biologically superior master race and that other races, Jews in particular, were genetically inferior and responsible for all of Germany's problems.

Hitler's answer to "the Jewish problem" was to exterminate the entire Jewish population of Europe. This plan to murder all Jews came to be known as "the Final Solution."

Chapter 3

TAKEN OVER

Celia entered her hometown—and immediately ducked down. Police and local farmers were going street to street, smashing windows and breaking down doors, as if their whole purpose was to do as much damage as possible. Celia watched her non-Jewish neighbors barging into stores and coming out with armfuls of silverware, clothes, clocks, and other goods. She recognized some of the looters. These were people she'd known all her life, and now they were destroying Jewish homes and businesses.

She hid for the rest of the day. At night, when the looting stopped and people dispersed, she quietly ran home. But something was wrong. Her house and several streets around it were surrounded by a wooden fence topped with barbed wire. The door to her house was wide open. Soldiers were coming and going.

Celia's stomach dropped. The Nazis had taken over her town and her home.

But where's my family? she wondered.

Carefully, she circled around her house and approached a small two-room storage shack at the back of the property. Inside, she found her parents, brothers, and sisters. Her older sisters were married with little children of their own, and everyone was squeezed together in the tiny space. Her parents and siblings were so relieved to see Celia alive. They immediately encircled her in their arms and flooded her with hugs and kisses.

"While you were away at school," her mother, Liba, said, "the Germans marched in and turned our part of town into a ghetto."

Celia knew the word *ghetto*. It meant an isolated section of a city or town where Nazis forced Jews to live in horribly crowded conditions, with no access to food or medicine. Celia's parents said the Germans had squeezed nearly nineteen hundred Jews into the Szarkowszczyzna ghetto.

"The overcrowding is unbearable," Liba said. "There's practically no food, and we're not allowed to send children to school or do our usual jobs. Everyone must work for the Nazis."

"What kind of work?" Celia asked.

"Whatever dirty jobs they have," her mother said. "We clean

their toilets. We wash their clothes. We scrub their jeeps, sweep the floors of their quarters, feed their horses, mop their stables—whatever they tell us to do."

The two-room shack was freezing cold. There was no stove or fireplace. That night, Celia and her brothers and sisters slept close together to stay warm.

The next day, Celia walked the streets and could not believe what she was seeing. Jews were imprisoned like animals behind the barbed-wire fence. Like many others in Poland, she had heard the Nazi propaganda that Jews were supposedly less than human. But she had always thought that one day the Nazis' horrible speeches would stop and their harsh words would vanish into thin air. She never imagined it would come to this—that Jew-hatred could look like this.

Nazis saw themselves as "the master race"—better than everyone else. Not only did they think themselves superior, but they also treated with cruelty anyone they judged to be inferior. Their victims included religious minorities such as Jehovah's Witnesses and ethnic groups such as Roma people, who were sometimes called by the pejorative name "Gypsies." The Nazis also singled out for cruel treatment people with disabilities, homosexual people, and anyone else they decided was an "enemy of Germany." The Nazis brutalized all of them.

But it was clear now to Celia that the Nazis had something worse in mind for Jews. Something much worse.

She walked back to the beautiful house that had once been her family home. Inside, she found people crammed into every room. The soldiers had turned the Cimmers' house into an overcrowded barrack for Jewish prisoners.

And Celia and her family were now the Nazis' servants.

GHETTOS

By first isolating Jewish people in ghettos, the Nazis had an easier time deporting them to their deaths at concentration camps, death camps, and other murder sites. Inside the ghettos, Nazi soldiers helped themselves to anything of value that the Jews possessed, beat them with clubs, and shot them at random.

Starvation was one of many ways Nazis murdered Jews. They did allow trucks to bring a little food into the ghettos, but they limited the amount Jews could eat to only four hundred calories per day, the equivalent of two slices of bread. Later, they reduced the amount to two hundred calories per day. No one could live on so little food, and prisoners tried to stay alive by trading with people outside the ghettos and smuggling food in through holes in fences and walls.

Still, even for people with something to trade, food was scarce, and the death rate from starvation and lack of medical care was staggering. When Nazi forces took over Poland in 1941, there were more than three million Jews in the country. The Nazis established about seven hundred ghettos in Poland alone, and within a few years, a half million Jews had died from starvation and disease.

Chapter 4

TURNING POINT

"Get up! Now!"

Each morning, soldiers showed up at the little two-room shack. They banged on the door with the butts of their rifles and demanded that Celia's family make them breakfast.

One snowy morning, the soldiers ordered Celia and her family to clear the roads.

"We have no shovels," Celia said.

"Use your hands!" a soldier yelled at her. It was now the winter of 1941. There were hardly any coats or sweaters to be found anywhere. The Nazis had taken them.

Celia's mother was forced to cook for Nazi administrators in the ghetto. They never paid her, but now and then they gave her a sack of flour for her own use. Liba added water and baked as many loaves of bread as the sack of flour would allow. She gave the bread first to her family, then whatever was left over she distributed to needy people in the ghetto. It was hard to decide who to give the bread to, since everyone was hungry.

Usually, she looked to see who was thinnest or at greatest risk of starving. To increase the number of loaves, Liba added more and more water to the dough, until it was a thin gruel barely fit for baking.

Celia marveled at how her mother worked day and night to feed her family and still found enough energy to care for others. She marveled, too, at how her mother bore with dignity the Nazis' abuses and insults.

As winter progressed, food became harder to find. Every day, Celia saw people fall to the ground and die from starvation.

Hunger drove people to extremes. The Cimmer family's two-room shack had a window that faced one of the barbed-wire fences. At night, Celia sat by the window and watched prisoners cut holes in the wire and crawl out to hunt for food in neighboring towns. Guards stationed at street corners caught most of the escapees and shot them on the spot.

Those guards don't know the people they're killing, Celia thought. *Why do they hate them so much?* She remembered her former friend who'd slammed the door in her face, and Celia could not think of one reasonable explanation for such hatred. With each passing day, she felt like someone had taken a giant eraser and was rubbing out the picture of her world until it was barely recognizable anymore.

Celia discovered that Nazi brutality took different forms. Some days, she saw guards cut the beards off religious Jewish men and beat them. Other days, she witnessed guards rounding up Jews who wore glasses or carried books. For the crime of looking too intelligent, they were shot. One day, she heard guards announce there was work for twenty-five bookkeepers. People who were bookkeepers volunteered. There was no work for bookkeepers. The announcement had been another excuse to round up Jews and shoot them.

Each week, Nazis in charge of the ghetto posted edicts—rules—that Jews were required to follow. One edict required all Jews to wear white cloth armbands with a yellow star sewn on. A few non-Jews came and went in the ghetto—people who were making deliveries or worked for the Nazi administrators—and when soldiers looked for Jews to humiliate or torture, the armband made it easier to identify them.

One edict required Jews to hand over any valuables they might still possess, such as watches, bicycles, radios, dishes, and coats. Yet another edict outlawed religious services. Celia's family was not particularly religious, but many other Jewish families in the ghetto were. On Friday nights, to honor the Sabbath, some families took great chances by saying prayers and lighting candles in the dark, with blankets covering windows to hide the candlelight.

Another edict forbade Jews to walk on the sidewalks. They could walk only in the gutters, and when a German approached, they had to remove their caps as a sign of respect.

The Nazis didn't kill everyone, as there were still tasks to be done. Healthy men and women were needed to dig ditches, repair buildings and roads, perform secretarial functions, cook, and clean. Still, to be chosen for any of these assignments was no guarantee of survival. Every Jew in the ghetto knew that sooner or later, the Germans would kill them all.

Children were not spared. Police conducted house-to-house searches. They rounded up any children they found and sent them away in trucks. The children were never seen again. When the sound of soldiers' boots echoed on the street outside their tiny shack, Celia's mother hid her youngest child, Slava, under a blanket.

To feed and protect their children, Liba and Shmuel sold nearly everything they had and used the money to buy whatever little bit of food was available. To keep their children warm, they lined their coats with newspaper for better insulation. To keep them learning, they homeschooled them with stories and lessons from their own school days.

Despite their best efforts, Shmuel and Liba ran out of food, money, and ideas, and they could no longer protect their children. They sat them down and said words that brought tears to the eyes of Celia and her siblings.

"My children," Shmuel said, "we have done our best to keep the family together and alive. Now it is you who must help us."

"Starting today," Liba explained, "each of us will have to do more. You will have to find your own work." Then she cried from shame. What kind of mother tells her children they have to fend for themselves?

Celia and her siblings did not blame their parents. They knew how hard they had tried to keep the family together. They looked at one another as the seriousness of the moment sank in. From now on, they would have to take responsibility for themselves. The older siblings in particular would have to prove to the Germans that they could do meaningful work, that they were more valuable alive than dead.

Celia's youngest sister, Slava, said she would stay and help her older sisters with their little children.

Celia's brothers, Hershke and Zalman, confirmed their plan to join the partisans. They preferred taking their chances working with the resistance.

"We don't know where the partisans are, but we'll find a way to communicate with them," Zalman said.

"And soon," Hershke added.

Celia was intrigued by the idea of joining the partisans, but she knew her brothers wouldn't let her. So she made a plan of her own for finding work.

"You know that police building where the Nazis have their headquarters?" she said. "I heard they need Jews there to clean and do office work. Maybe they have a job for me."

These matters were discussed as calmly as possible, but just below the surface was a cruel message: to avoid starving, the family was being forced to break up.

PARTISANS

Partisans were underground fighting groups dedicated to disrupting Nazi operations and bringing help to the Nazis' victims. Partisans operated in Nazi-occupied cities, but many more operated outside the cities in densely wooded areas. There were about 30,000 Jewish partisans during World War II. A large percentage were teenagers, and about one in ten were women.

Some partisan units were composed completely of Jewish fighters. Many of these Jewish fighters had escaped from ghettos and concentration camps and formed their own partisan groups. One particularly famous Jewish partisan group was led by three brothers with the last name Bielski. Before the war, the Bielskis had been a farming family in Belorussia. At the start of the Holocaust, the three Bielski brothers succeeded in building a community of partisans in swampy sections of the forests of Belorussia. Under the brothers' protection, more than twelve hundred Jews survived the war.

Other partisan units were composed of non-Jewish fighters or had only a few Jews among them. The partisan unit that

Celia's brothers, Zalman and Hershke, joined (and that Celia would eventually join) was a Soviet unit with very few Jewish members.

Both Jewish and non-Jewish partisans fought against the Nazis. Jews serving in non-Jewish partisan units, however, still had a hard time, as they often faced antisemitism from their own members.

Chapter 5

LIKE A ZOMBIE

The next day, Celia put on her best dress, scrubbed her face, cleaned her shoes, and presented herself at Nazi headquarters. An officer looked her up and down.

"We need waitresses to work in our dining room," he said. "Show me your hands."

She held out her hands and turned them up and down.

"You seem clean enough," the officer said. "Well-mannered, too—and you're pretty. Okay, you get the job. But keep your fingernails clean and trimmed and bathe every day before coming here. We don't want any dirty, smelly Jews serving our officers."

Celia hated the idea of serving meals to Nazi officers. These were the people who issued orders for Jews to be tortured and killed. Still, she calculated that being a waitress would give her certain advantages. For one, she would be around leftover food, which she could smuggle out for her family. Plus, she might overhear conversations and gather useful information, such as when the Germans were planning to liquidate the ghetto. *Liquidate* was a word all Jews in the ghetto knew and feared. It meant killing every Jewish man, woman, and child. With some advance notice, maybe some people could be saved.

Celia thanked the officer, and the next day she showed up for work. For a while, the position turned out as she had hoped. She was able to save scraps of food, and now and then she overheard a discussion that provided useful information.

Then something happened that turned a useful job into a nightmare.

The Polish commandant of the ghetto was a tall man who, before being appointed commandant, had been a local bully with no real authority. After his appointment, he became a tyrant. He carried a riding crop and frequently clicked his heels together and raised his arm in the Hitler salute. He was one of the many cruel people for whom Hitler, with his manic hatred of Jews, was a role model.

Years before, Celia recalled, this same local man had wanted to buy her parents' house. Shmuel and Liba declined his offer, and ever since then, the man carried a grudge against them.

Now, with his newly acquired power, he saw a chance to get his revenge.

One night, he sent two policemen to Celia's home. "We have orders to arrest you," they said, and marched her to the commandant's office.

She looked around the room and saw a photo of Hitler hanging above the desk. The commandant's jacket and cap were draped over a clothing rack by the door. The man himself was in his shirtsleeves, sitting on a big wooden armchair with his arms crossed. Celia stood and waited for him to say something. She was frightened but kept her expression neutral and tried not to show her fear.

"I have good news for you," the commandant said. "From now on, you get to be my girlfriend. You get to live with me. Of course, you will clean my house and do everything I tell you to do. But in exchange, I will spare your life."

Celia felt sick, but she wasn't going to allow this bully to think he could intimidate her. She shook her head. "No thanks."

"Then I'll kill you. I've done it before. Ask anyone."

Celia knew him for the skunk he was. Since waitressing for the Germans, she'd heard him at meals, bragging to ghetto personnel around the table about how close he was with the Nazi higher-ups, how much they trusted him—all lies. It was clear to her the Germans tolerated him only because they needed him to oversee the ghetto.

And it was also clear why Hitler was such a hero to a person like him. Putting on a Nazi uniform gave him legal authority to do whatever he wanted. That included hurting people like Celia if she failed to offer him the respect he thought he was owed.

"Go ahead," Celia said. "Kill me. I'm not going to do it."

The commandant was shocked by Celia's refusal. Defying a Nazi officer was a crime punishable by death. It also made the commandant look foolish in front of his men. He jumped up out of his chair and pointed a finger at Celia. "You'll soon change your mind!" he yelled.

He ordered his officers to march Celia to a stone room in the basement of the building. Celia had heard about this room. It was a torture chamber, often used by the police to force Jews into telling them where they hid their valuables. The room had only one small window, and the walls were made of thick stone. No one outside could hear the screams.

The officers shackled Celia to metal rings screwed into the

floor. Then they took turns beating her with rubber hoses. After several hours, she lost consciousness.

In the morning, icy daylight filtered into her cell through the barred window. Celia woke to find her hands and legs stuck to the floor. During the night, the officers had thrown buckets of water over her. In the cold night air, the water had frozen and glued her skin to the stone floor. She looked up and saw the commandant standing over her.

"Today, I will shoot you," he said. He ordered his men to scrape her off the floor and march her to the nearby Jewish cemetery.

And now I'm going to die, Celia thought, resigned to her fate.

The route to the cemetery ran parallel to the barbed wire fence that surrounded the ghetto. Behind the fence, Jewish prisoners had assembled. They'd heard about Celia's arrest and knew she was being marched to her death. Celia's family was there, and as the police passed by with Celia in handcuffs, her family tossed whatever money and jewelry they still had over the fence.

"Here!" Liba and Shmuel cried out. "Take these gifts!"

"She's just a child!" Celia's siblings cried out, frantic and desperate. "Please let her go!"

The bribes and pleas had no effect. The police walked on,

holding Celia up under her arms. She tried not to look at her family. She didn't want them to see how terrified she was.

When they arrived at the cemetery, the police marched Celia before the commandant, who stood with the morning sun in his face, his uniform sharply pressed, his medals shining.

"This is your last chance," he told her. "Beg me to forgive you and agree to be my girlfriend, and I'll call off the execution. You'll see. I can be a compassionate man."

Celia looked at the police. They were locals. Some of their children had been Celia's classmates. These men could stop this from happening. Where was *their* compassion?

"I won't do it," she told the commandant.

He whispered an order to his men. They drew their pistols and pointed them at Celia. They fired the guns. The explosion was as loud as a lightning bolt hitting her head. It was the last thing Celia heard. Then everything went black.

When she came to, she was on the ground in the cemetery, surrounded by people from the ghetto. Blood dripped from her ears. The commandant had told his men to shoot but avoid killing her. The bullets had passed within inches of her head, causing hearing damage that would last the rest of her life. The prisoners lifted her up and carried her home. Celia fell weeping into her mother's arms.

"You're safe now," Liba said, holding her terrified daughter and rocking her back and forth like a baby.

Years later, Celia described that after being nearly murdered in the cemetery, she had a hard time thinking clearly. "I lost touch with everyday reality," she explained. "I just stumbled about—like a zombie."

It took weeks for Celia to recover. While some of her hearing returned, nothing could erase what she'd been through.

Where is my childhood? she wondered.

Before the war, before her school was bombed, before she was nearly murdered, life had followed a familiar pattern. She drifted happily along from breakfast to classes, homework, play, and then sleep. That was her young girl's life. She always knew that becoming more mature was bound to happen.

But this was not merely the natural process of changing from a child to a young adult. It was the world itself that had changed. The world wasn't what she thought, something fixed and dependable. She saw now there were forces at work over which she had no control, and that change could happen in much bigger, frightening ways. It was as though she had discovered a basic truth about life that required her to grow up fast and say a quick goodbye to childish things.

With rest and the love of her family, eventually Celia

regained enough strength to return to work. She had no choice. Her family would have no food if she didn't go back to the Nazis' dining hall. Once again, she put on her best dress, pinched her cheeks to make them rosy, walked to Nazi headquarters, and resumed serving meals to her tormentors.

THE HOLOCAUST

Holocaust, from the Greek word meaning "burnt offering," refers to the fires of concentration camp crematorium ovens, where bodies of murdered Jews were burned to ashes.

The Holocaust evolved during the years Nazi Germany occupied much of Europe. It began in 1933, when Germany built its first concentration camp, Dachau, and ended in 1945 with the conclusion of the war. The Holocaust is usually defined as the systematic, state-sponsored murder of more than six million Jewish men, women, and children by Nazi Germany and its allies. Other ethnic, religious, and national groups were targeted for imprisonment or worse by the Nazi party, but of all their so-called enemies, only the Jewish population was targeted by the Nazis for complete destruction.

The Nazis carried out the murder of Europe's Jewish population through brutality, mass shootings, poison gassings, and specially designed killing centers.

The Holocaust is also sometimes referred to as "the Shoah," the Hebrew word for *catastrophe*.

Chapter 6

CHOICELESS CHOICE

Winter ended, and the harsh weather gave way to a mild spring. One warm day in June 1942, Celia was serving meals in the officers' dining hall. The doors and windows were open, and a breeze wafted around the room, carrying conversations through the air. Celia overheard something that nearly made her drop a stack of plates. Officers were discussing July 18 as the date for liquidating the ghetto.

Celia finished her work, ran home, and reported to her parents what she'd heard. Shmuel was a member of the ghetto's Judenrat, the council of Jewish leaders, and he hurried to bring the information to them. The leaders agreed that, in light of this terrible news, everyone who could escape should do so immediately. Word spread and triggered a stampede of people desperate to get away. Those who could not run—mostly the old and disabled—were left behind. The others ran to the ghetto fence, cut holes in the barbed wire, and scattered into the nearby woods.

In their two-room shack, the Cimmer family was preparing to run.

"Go!" Shmuel shouted to his wife and children. Then he sat down on the one chair in their tiny shack and folded his hands. Celia and her mother and siblings were confused. What was he doing?

"Papa, you're coming, aren't you? You must come!" Celia pleaded.

Shmuel shook his head. "I'm staying," he said, and gave no explanation. "Go! Now!"

Celia had heard a rumor that prisoners were planning to burn down the ghetto rather than leave it to the Nazis. Her father was in terrible danger if he stayed. But there was nothing she could do to change his mind. Celia hugged her father goodbye and grabbed Slava by the hand. They hurried to the fence, ducked through a hole in the barbed wire, and ran. They did not look back and had no idea if the rest of their family had escaped. The sisters kept running.

"Celia!" a voice shouted.

Celia turned around. Standing only a few yards away was a boy her age. He looked familiar. The boy was holding a rifle. He raised the rifle and pointed it at her. Then she remembered. He was a non-Jewish classmate from Druya. Now he wore a soldier's uniform and was about to kill her. At that moment, a thought crossed her mind. *This skinny little schoolboy looks so silly, dressed up like a soldier.* Celia remembered her other classmate from Druya, the so-called best friend who turned her away the night of the bombing. How many classmates wanted her dead? Nothing made sense anymore.

The boy pulled the trigger. *Click.* Nothing happened. The rifle had jammed. Celia and Slava turned toward the woods and continued running.

Just as they were about to rush into the woods, Celia saw a man from the ghetto carrying two bundles. One bundle seemed to be pants and shirts and other clothing. The second bundle was crying—a small child wrapped in a coat. The man stumbled and both bundles fell to the ground. Guards from the ghetto were chasing him and getting closer. In his haste to get away, by mistake the man grabbed the bundle of clothing and ran, leaving his child behind. Celia did not look back again. She and Slava hurried into the woods, ducking under tree branches, pushing aside bushes and vines.

When they had put a mile or more between themselves and the ghetto, they rested. Over the tops of trees, they saw the nighttime sky aglow with a pulsing red cloud. Szarkowszczyzna was burning. The Jews had made good on their plan to burn down the town. Celia thought of her many family members still in the ghetto, including her father. Had they escaped? Were any of them still alive?

"We have to keep going," she told Slava.

The two sisters ran, dodging rocks and fallen trees. Here and there, they saw other escapees from the ghetto looking for places to hide.

An hour later, the sisters arrived at the edge of a swamp. The murky water was thick with sludge from dead leaves and foul-smelling mulch. Tall reeds loomed up from the dark mud. Celia and Slava held hands, waded in, and crouched down until only their heads were above water. The muddy water was so cold it stung, and the sisters clung together for warmth. Beneath the swamp water, leeches smelled their flesh and attacked. The worms burrowed into their clothes and bit their legs and backs. No matter how bad the pain, Celia and Slava pressed their lips together and stayed silent.

Celia peered out from the reeds. On the shore, German guards and Polish police ran past, yelling at fleeing prisoners—"Stop!"—and shooting at them. Celia and Slava saw many escapees fall to the ground. In the years to come, historians would estimate that Nazi forces that night killed six hundred prisoners from the ghetto. Nine hundred others managed to escape.

Police informed farmers living in the area that the hunt was on for escaped Jews. It was easy to tempt the farmers into becoming collaborators and joining the search. Most were poor and uneducated and greedy for bottles of vodka, sacks of salt, boxes of food, and other rewards they would collect from police for every captured Jew. The farmers had heard that in the seams of their clothing some Jews sewed watches, rings, earrings, money, and other valuables. Murdering a Jew might just bring them these added riches.

The search parties combed the woods. Celia and Slava stayed crouched in the freezing swamp. Hours passed.

Morning finally came, and the shooting and yelling faded away. In the west, the sky was the dull color of old clothing, the air heavy and damp. Water dripped from trees onto the surface of the swamp, creating ripples that broke apart on the tall reeds. But the mildness of the morning could not erase from the sisters' minds the horror of what they had witnessed.

When all was quiet, Celia and Slava crawled toward shore. They climbed up onto the riverbank and huddled close together, hugging to stay warm and pulling leeches off each other's arms and legs.

Slowly, other escapees from the ghetto came out of hiding. A small group formed. No one knew where to go or what to do next. Celia looked frantically through the crowd but saw none of her family. From far away, she heard the sound of a jeep approaching. Soldiers were making an announcement through portable loudspeakers.

"Men and women from the ghetto!" the soldiers called out. "Save yourselves. Any of you still in hiding, if you give yourselves up, you will be allowed to relocate. The Glubok ghetto is nearby. You will be given work. You will be given food and a place to sleep. No questions asked."

The escapees were not fooled. They knew that sooner or later the Glubok ghetto, too, would be liquidated. But what choice did they have? If they stayed in the woods, they would freeze to death when the weather turned cold or eventually die of hunger. Under such conditions, there was no good choice, only this bad choice or that bad choice—what Holocaust educators today call a choiceless choice.

One by one, more escapees came out of hiding. The group started walking to the Glubok ghetto, seven miles away. Celia and Slava joined them. A few prisoners refused to go to another ghetto and preferred to take their chances in hiding. Although Celia did not know it at the time, among those who stayed in hiding were her two older brothers, Zalman and

Hershke. The brothers made their way deeper into the surrounding forest, determined to join the partisans.

Some hours later, the group of escapees arrived at the ghetto. Guards opened the gates and herded everyone inside. Celia held her sister's hand as they walked down one street after another, stopping strangers and asking, "We're looking for our relatives. Do you know the Cimmer family?"

Eventually, they were directed to a small room in a dilapidated wooden building, where they found their mother, two of their sisters, and their sisters' children. They had also been rounded up with the other escapees in the woods. The joy of the reunion did not last long, as the conversation soon turned to who had perished and who was still alive. Celia tried to remember the many people who had once been her extended family. If she included in-laws, cousins, aunts and uncles, and nephews and nieces, the number was very large. She was looking at a small handful who were still alive.

The first thing Liba did was get Celia and Slava out of their dirty, wet clothes. There was no bathtub or running water. She wiped them down as best she could with rags. Liba collected some dry clothing from her other daughters and handed it over to Celia and Slava. Then she said something that shocked the two sisters.

"Why did you come here?" Liba yelled. "You should have stayed in hiding! I don't want you here!"

Celia understood her mother's anger. Liba wanted Celia and Slava to live. The odds of survival were better in hiding than here in a ghetto.

Liba broke down and cried. "You know I love you," she said, "but you must go away. Yesterday, the Nazis rounded up two thousand young people here in the ghetto and killed them all. You have to escape. At least someone from our family should survive."

Celia looked at her sister, but Slava shook her head. "I'm not going," she said. Young Slava walked across the splintered floor and took her mother's hand.

Celia stood alone on one side of the room. The rest of her family stood huddled together on the other side. "How can I leave you?" Celia cried. "How can I leave my family? Can't we all run away together?"

Liba pointed her chin at Celia's older sisters, holding their little children. "I won't leave them," she said. "Celia, there's something you need to know. Your father is dead. He was killed by the Nazis after we ran from the ghetto. Some neighbors are here. They saw it."

My father is dead, Celia told herself. She tried putting the words together in some other arrangement in her head that would make them mean something else. Maybe he was missing, or he had escaped to some other town. Maybe her mother meant anything other than what she said. No, there was no magical way to make death into something else.

Years later, Celia reflected that her father must have stayed back because he knew the Nazis would catch everyone who escaped. He had probably told himself that when they did, they would kill them all, and he didn't want to see that. *That's why he stayed*, Celia thought to herself. *He didn't want to watch his family die. He preferred to stay back and die first.*

Liba walked over and wrapped her arms around Celia. "Okay, stay a while," she said softly. "These will be our last days together. Then you must escape."

How am I going to do that? Celia wondered. *Nazi guards aren't going to let a Jew just walk out of here. Escape is impossible.*

COLLABORATORS

As the war progressed, Nazi Germany increased its efforts to murder every Jew in Europe. Those who voluntarily aided the Germans were called collaborators.

In 1941, after eastern Poland came under German control, many Polish people chose to become collaborators. Some did so because they hated Jews, others did so because they believed the Nazi propaganda that Jews had to die, and still others did so because they wanted to win favors from local Nazi authorities. Collaborators included police, railroad personnel, town officials, farmers, shopkeepers, and anyone else willing to hunt down Jews in hiding. Collaborators existed in every Nazi-occupied country and on all levels of society, from the very rich to the very poor. Celia and her family had to be on guard against collaborators not only from Poland but also from the surrounding regions, such as Ukraine, Lithuania, and Belorussia (known today as Belarus).

Collaborators received rewards for turning in Jews. They also actively participated in stealing their property. In some cases, particularly in the small towns, collaborators took part in murdering their Jewish neighbors.

By the end of the war, three million Polish Jews—90 percent of Poland's prewar Jewish population—had been murdered, one of the highest percentages in any European country. The slaughter would not have been possible without the cooperation of collaborators.

Some non-Jewish individuals in Nazi-occupied Europe risked their lives to save Jews, but they were a very small minority.

Chapter 7

CHARADES

Some time after Celia arrived in the Glubok ghetto, a tall young man with floppy brown hair, wearing a yellow Jewish star on his jacket, came to the ghetto's gate. He kept his cap low over his face. The guard assumed he was one more Jew turning himself in with the other escapees and pushed him through the gate.

The young man was a Polish Christian boy named Piotr Belevich. Piotr was born one year before Celia and lived with his older brother and parents, Jan and Maria, on their family's farm. At age ten, Piotr had attended the same primary school as Celia in Szarkowszczyzna. It took Piotr many hours traveling by horse-drawn wagon to get from his farm to the school. To help Piotr avoid the long ride, Jan and Maria asked Celia's parents if they would rent out a room for their son. Shmuel and Liba were pleased to have Piotr live with them. He was a polite boy who never objected to helping with chores, and their house was big. Renting out a spare room was not an inconvenience.

After living in the same home with Celia and spending so much time together, Piotr developed a crush on her. Even now, years later, he still had strong feelings for her.

Piotr was secretly a member of the local partisan group, and he had used his connections to help Celia's two brothers escape arrest and join the partisans. When he found out that Celia was alive and in the Glubok ghetto, he came up with a plan to help her escape as well.

Piotr walked down the streets of the ghetto, asking if anyone knew the Cimmer family. Eventually, he found them. Celia was amazed to see her old friend.

"I can't believe you're here," she said. "Why would you sneak into a ghetto?"

"I'm here to get you out," he told her.

Celia must have understood this was Piotr's way of expressing his affection for her, but this was not the time for such distractions. "It's impossible to get out of here," she said. "Jews are not allowed to leave. We'll be shot."

"I brought false papers," Piotr said, and he showed her the documents. "The guard will think we were delivering something for the Nazis. Then we'll walk out of here. You can do it. I believe in you. You can do anything."

Celia knew the Nazis would shoot them on the spot. But someday soon the Nazis were going to shoot everyone in the ghetto anyway. Stay or go? Choiceless choice.

Well, if I really am daring like my mother, she thought, *this would be the time to find out.*

Celia agreed to Piotr's plan. They used pins to remove the stitches holding the yellow stars to their jackets. Celia hugged her mother and sisters with all her might. She and Piotr walked to the gates of the ghetto. Piotr again pulled his cap low so the guard would not recognize him. He showed his counterfeit papers to the guard. Celia held her breath. The guard looked the papers over, then waved them through the gate. Celia and Piotr walked out of the ghetto.

Celia couldn't believe what they had just done. They were out.

She and Piotr walked in silence for about an hour. It was August in a part of Poland where the summer wind was warm and carried the scent of wheat fields and river water. There were no buildings around them, nothing to tarnish the view of sky and trees and fields. Off to the side, Celia saw farmers tilling fields with oxen, adjusting the plow left or right to keep the furrows straight. Birds flew by overhead.

Sadness comes and sadness goes, but the goodness of nature will always be there, Celia thought. She was quiet for a while, savoring the moment. She and Piotr had just won a victory over the largest, most deadly enemy the world had ever known. Two kids from small towns, with no weapons, no money, no powerful contacts in business or government, had pulled a fast one on Hitler and his so-called superior Aryan race.

They heard the clip-clop of horses behind them. Celia looked back and saw two men coming their way in a wagon. She grabbed Piotr by the arm.

"I know those men," she whispered. "They're Nazi officials from the ghetto. If they recognize me, they'll shoot me for trying to escape. Then they'll shoot you for trying to save a Jew."

"Just smile," Piotr said. "Leave the rest to me."

The wagon pulled up, but the officials made no indication of recognizing Celia. "Hop in," the driver said.

Celia and Piotr had no choice. No one refused a free lift unless they had something to hide. They climbed in, and the wagon set out. Piotr kept the officials amused by chatting and joking. Celia did her best to smile and not show how terrified she was. She admired the way Piotr could remain so calm. *He's not so bad-looking, either. Under other circumstances . . .* she started to think, then stopped. This was not the time.

A few hours later, they heard music playing in the distance. One of the local villages was holding a dance.

"We must stop and have some fun!" insisted the driver, and he steered his horses toward the music. Celia and Piotr exchanged glances. If they were going to survive, they had to go along with whatever happened.

All night, Celia pretended to be a Polish Christian girl out with her Nazi friends for an evening of fun. The room was filled with local collaborators, every one of them committed to the Nazi cause. Celia had to put on the performance of a lifetime. She smiled and sang as though she wasn't surrounded by Jew-hating neighbors. She behaved as though there were no war, no starvation, no wholesale slaughter of Jews. She laughed and danced as though so many of her family and friends had not been murdered by the likes of these people with whom she was pretending to have a good time.

When the sun rose over the horizon and the dance finally ended, Celia, Piotr, and the ghetto officials climbed back onto the wagon and drove away. Eventually, they arrived at Piotr's family farm. Celia and Piotr jumped off, waved a friendly farewell, and watched as the ghetto officers drove off down the road and out of sight.

Celia let out a big sigh and shed a few tears. The charade was over.

Another one was about to begin.

Chapter 8

NERVES OF STEEL

"It's only for a few days," Piotr promised his parents.

His plan to hide Celia on their farm had his mother and father terrified. Police and other local collaborators were conducting searches of homes and farms every day, and anyone found hiding a Jew was shot.

Piotr promised his parents that he would hide Celia so well that the Nazis would never find her. Piotr's parents finally agreed, provided Celia agreed to stay out of sight the entire day. She could come out for a little while, they said, but only at night.

For Celia, this was practically a miracle. She knew most Polish people would never help a Jew. How wonderful to discover that some, such as Piotr and his parents, were willing to do so even at great personal risk. What a surprise to discover that there were still kind people in a world where kindness was in such short supply.

Piotr was facing a serious challenge. Where could he hide

Celia so that no one would ever find her? Attics and closets were out. Those were the first places soldiers would search. Under the filthy ground of the barn, on the other hand, might work. Cow and chicken manure made excellent camouflage. Even Nazis looking for Jews would not want to go poking around in a pile of animal dung.

Piotr waited until the farm workers were gone for the day, then he took a shovel and started digging into the dirt floor of the barn. Soon he had created a hole just big enough for Celia to crawl in. Once she was lying in the hole, Piotr nailed several wooden boards together into a plank. He positioned the plank over the hole and shoveled sand and manure on top. It was the perfect hiding place.

And it was the most horrible hiding place imaginable. This was the harvest season, and the farm was crowded with workers. On days when the workers came early and stayed late, Celia had to stay in that hole twenty-four hours a day. She could not move or make a sound. She had to remain motionless, her arms folded across her chest like a mummy. She was so scared she couldn't sleep. After only a few days, she was starving, exhausted, and every part of her body ached from lack of movement.

On days when the farm workers left early, Piotr pulled her

out and gave her a bowl of water to wash her face. She walked around the barn, stretching her aching arms and legs. Piotr gave her a cup of soup, a mouthful of cabbage, or whatever he'd been able to find. Giving her even that little bit of food was a big sacrifice. Nazi authorities forced farmers such as the Belevich family to hand over nearly everything they grew. Harvests went first to feed the German army, and only a little remained for the Polish people. To feed Celia, Piotr shared with her what he had kept for himself.

Then Celia took a deep breath, let it out, and climbed back into the hole. Piotr again positioned the wooden plank over the hole and covered it over with straw and manure.

Many years later, when Celia told her story to an interviewer, she explained what it felt like to hide in a hole for weeks at a time.

"Being alone, exposed to cold and wet, to rats and worms and always hungry, I didn't think much at all," she said. "When the harvest was finished and there weren't any workers in the barn, Piotr brought me a candle made from a potato. He took a potato and jammed a stick into it. He wrapped a little cotton on the end, then dipped the cotton in a cup of oil. When he lit the cotton, I was able to read by the light. He brought me books, and reading helped me pass the time. But think? I tried not to think. It was too painful to think, to hope that maybe someone from my family was still alive. I couldn't cry, either. There wasn't one tear that came out of me. I was just numb."

While Celia was hiding on Piotr's farm, her remaining family members were forty miles away in Glubok, facing ordeals of their own.

RIGHTEOUS AMONG THE NATIONS

"Righteous Among the Nations" is one of Israel's highest civilian honors. It is a title awarded by Yad Vashem, Israel's leading Holocaust museum and archive, to non-Jews who, for purely unselfish reasons, risked their lives to save Jews from being murdered by Nazi Germany or its collaborators during the Holocaust.

In Nazi-occupied territories, the task of rescuing Jews was difficult and dangerous. Anyone found hiding a Jew in their home or on their property would be sentenced to die.

To qualify as a Righteous Among the Nations, the nominated person must have offered repeated or substantial assistance to Jews, without expecting any financial reward or payment in return.

As of January 1, 2022, the honor had been given to 28,217 people. Nearly one quarter of the awards were given to Polish citizens. The list of Righteous Among the Nations is not comprehensive.

Only a fraction of those who unselfishly helped Jews have been identified. It is estimated that hundreds of thousands of others helped Jews during the Holocaust.

In October 1998, the Israeli government recognized Celia's friend Piotr Belevich as Righteous Among the Nations. His name is displayed with others so honored on a memorial wall in the Yad Vashem museum.

Chapter 9

CRAWLING TO SAFETY

In the ghettos, Nazi officials forced Jews to carry bricks, repair roads, dig trenches, and do other back-breaking labor twelve hours or more each day. Prisoners who could not do the work were either deported to concentration camps or marched to nearby woods and shot. Periodically, Nazi officers went through the Glubok ghetto looking for anyone too old, too sick, or too young to do manual labor.

Celia's youngest sister, Slava, spent most of her time hiding.

At night, Celia's mother, Liba, was haunted by dreams of her children and grandchildren being killed. After months of hunger and fear for their lives, she could no longer bear the strain. The constant tension drove her to a daring decision. She would somehow smuggle her remaining family out. She would find a way to get them to the town of Postavy, where her two surviving brothers lived.

This was the fall of 1942, harvest time. Once a week, a local Polish Christian farmer arrived at the ghetto with his horse-drawn wagon to deliver bales of hay, bags of vegetables, and other supplies. When no guards were watching, Liba walked up to the farmer and explained her family's situation.

"I have two brothers in the Postavy ghetto," Liba told him. "Will you please help us get there?"

To Liba's great relief, the farmer was sympathetic and agreed to help them escape. The plan was for Liba and her family to hide in his open-back wagon under a pile of hay. "I will be back next week," he said. "You must be ready."

On the day of their escape, the farmer drove his wagon into the ghetto at a leisurely pace, careful to not draw any attention. The guards knew him. He had been there many times. He nodded hello as his horse and wagon meandered down the streets of the ghetto. The horse clip-clopped along until the wagon arrived at the spot where the farmer had met Liba the week before. This time, Liba, Slava, and Dina and Miriam holding their babies, were all waiting for him.

When they were sure no one was watching, Liba and her family ran to the wagon and crawled under the hay. The farmer clicked his tongue, and the horse turned his wagon around and headed back toward the gates of the ghetto. The farmer nodded to the guard and drove slowly out.

Slava waited. When sounds from the ghetto had faded away,

she peeked out from under the hay and saw—heaven. No guards, no police, just a bright autumn day like the days she and her family had once known before there ever was a Hitler or a Nazi Germany. The wagon passed by sweet-smelling fields of wheat, rye, barley, and oats. Cows mooed in the distance, and the wagon rocked gently back and forth over the dirt road.

Slava could not remember the last time she felt such relief. She turned and looked at her mother, Liba, lying next to her, bits of straw sticking to her hair, and knew that she felt it, too. At least for this one day, they had been spared the horrible fate of so many other Jews.

The farmer drove for several hours, arriving at last to the town of Postavy. The Cimmer family climbed out of the wagon and stretched their arms and legs. Liba and her daughters kissed the farmer's hand. The farmer waved goodbye, flicked the horse's reins, and set out for home.

The Nazis had turned Postavy into a ghetto, and as in all ghettos, life for Jews in Postavy was miserable. So far, however, there had been no order to liquidate the ghetto. A sleepy guard raised the wooden barrier and let the Cimmers in. They walked down a packed dirt road and over a small wooden bridge that spanned a narrow stream. On the other side of the bridge, the road led them to the center of town. Rickety wooden fences separated one ramshackle house from the next. Some of the houses had brick facades, but bullets had loosened the bricks. The town lay in shambles.

None of the houses was more than two stories high, apart from a small empty church with a broken wooden dome. Everything was dusty gray, as though color had been leached from the town by Nazi decree. If someone wanted to design a place that made no impression and was easily forgotten, it might have looked like Postavy.

Liba had spent her early life here, and she knew where to go. It didn't take long for them to reach her brothers' home at the far end of the ghetto. When her brothers opened the door and saw their relatives, they wept and embraced them. They had lost hope of ever seeing Liba or her family again. The brothers quickly ushered everyone into their small house.

Slava looked around her uncles' home and was dismayed by how empty it was. She saw a splintered chair, a pockmarked table, an old wooden chest with a shirt hanging out, and not much else. No doubt the Nazis had already taken whatever they wanted, as they had done in the homes of Jews across Poland.

Her uncles had managed to keep a few blankets and save a

small supply of food. There was little to offer so many mouths, but for the first time in months, Slava and her family did not go to bed hungry.

The reunion did not stay happy for long. A short time later, in December 1942, word spread that the Germans were about to liquidate the Postavy ghetto. As Slava had already witnessed in her hometown ghetto, the rumor that everyone would soon be murdered triggered a rush to escape. When the sun set, Slava, her mother, and siblings followed others through holes in the barbed-wire fence and scrambled out.

This time, the Nazis were ready for the escapees and had positioned machine guns outside the fence. No sooner did Slava and her family crawl through the barbed wire than soldiers opened fire. Slava stifled a scream as she watched her sisters and their children fall to the ground.

Slava felt a tug. Liba was shot and clutching her daughter's shirt.

"Run, Slava. Go to Celia at Piotr's farm," Liba whispered. "Promise me." Then she died.

Slava felt a sharp sting on her leg. Then another at the top of her head. She was hit and fell to the ground. She looked up and saw Nazi soldiers running in her direction, pursuing prisoners.

Slava draped herself over her mother's body and pretended to be dead. The soldiers ran past her and kept running. Slava lay motionless, biting her tongue to not cry out from her wounds and not knowing when it would be safe to look up.

Hours later, a horse-drawn wagon arrived. Workers lifted Slava and threw her onto a pile of dead people in the back of the wagon. Then they drove on. The wagon entered a wooded area and stopped by an open pit. The drivers tossed bodies one by one from their wagon into the pit. When the wagon was empty, they rode away.

Slava lay in the pit, silent and still. The night was quiet, apart from shuffling sounds here and there in the pit. *Are there other Jews not yet dead*, she wondered, *or am I the only one still alive?* She was too frightened to ask out loud. Slowly, she crawled her way out of the pit. Her wounds throbbed. Blood dripped from her head and leg. She had lost her shoes and staggered away, barefoot and limping. She ran until she couldn't run anymore, then she slowed to a walk.

She walked through the cold night. An electric storm moved across the barren fields, flickering with lightning like flashes from a battery of rifles. When she could no longer walk, she fell to her knees and crawled. For days she inched her way forward, eating grass and leaves and sipping muddy water from puddles in the ground. Days later, Slava reached Piotr's farm. She dragged herself up to the farmhouse, lifted herself up, and peered cautiously through a window. There was Piotr sitting at a table, eating dinner with his family.

Seated with them at the table was her sister Celia.

Chapter 10

A TINY WITCH

Piotr looked up and saw Slava at the window. At first, he couldn't tell what he was looking at. A strange little person was staring at him, her clothes ripped and filthy, her face encrusted with dirt, and her hair sticking out like spikes on a porcupine. She looked like a tiny witch. Piotr looked closer and could hardly believe his eyes. It was Slava, and clearly she needed help. Piotr glanced at Celia, whose back was to the window. She didn't know that her sister was right there. Piotr's parents had also not seen Slava yet. He made a quick decision. He would not say a word to anyone unless he was sure Slava would live.

He excused himself from the table, as if he was going to the bathroom. He walked outside, picked Slava up in his arms, and carried her to the barn. Her body shook, frozen with cold and burning with fever.

Piotr dipped a wooden ladle into a bucket of water and gave her small sips to drink. He looked around the barn and found a pair of sheep shears and used them to cut away her frozen hair. Gently, he peeled off Slava's wet clothes and laid her on a wooden table. In a corner of the barn, a large kettle of animal fat hung over a wood fire. Piotr dipped a linen blanket into the kettle of warm fat and covered her body with the blanket. Slowly, the warm blanket raised her temperature.

When Slava finally stopped shivering, and when it seemed to Piotr she would survive, he returned to the farmhouse and told Celia and his family members that Slava was there. Celia dropped her spoon and ran to the barn. It had been months since she'd last seen Slava. She raced to her sister, leaned over her emaciated body, and carefully embraced her.

"It's not possible," Celia said. "How did you get here?"

The question was on the minds of Piotr and his family as well. The Postavy ghetto was forty miles away. It must have taken Slava days to reach the Belevich farm. Somehow, in the middle of winter, she had crossed rocky fields and a frozen river. If he wasn't seeing her with his own eyes, he would never have believed it. How did she survive such a journey?

Slava described the liquidation of the Postavy ghetto. She delivered the devastating news that their mother and the rest of their family were murdered trying to escape. She described holding Liba's hand as she lay dying, then getting shot, pretending to be dead, getting thrown from a wagon into a pit, and crawling out at night.

"I came to a small farmhouse," she said, "and at first, I didn't want to knock, looking the way I did. But I was cold and hungry, so I did. A woman opened the door. She was very nice to me. My feet were frozen. She gave me rags and pieces of rope, and I tied the rags around my feet. Then she gave me a slice of bread.

"I thanked her," Slava said, "and told her I was looking for the home of a boy named Piotr, who went to school with my sister. The woman pointed this way, so I walked all night. The following day, a man drove by in a wagon. Papa used to do business with people around here, so I thought maybe this man was friendly and could help me get here. I told him my name."

"Oh! Get in!" the man said.

Slava climbed slowly into the back of his wagon. Her body had never ached so much, but she worked hard to smile and appear like a normal person and not a half-dead Jew on the run. Slava wondered why the man had said nothing about her condition, until she turned around and smelled liquor on his breath. In his drunken delirium, the man mumbled something about the big reward he would get for turning in the daughter of a middle-class Jew.

This was no friend.

The horse-drawn wagon ambled down snow-covered roads. Slava waited for a chance to get away. They passed by a river that Slava recognized. She knew Piotr's farm was somewhere on the other side. Quietly and slowly, she rolled off the back of the wagon onto the ground and kept rolling until she reached the frozen river. The driver moved on, so drunk he didn't notice that his young passenger had escaped.

Slava crawled out onto the ice.

Crack!

The ice broke under her weight, and she dropped into the frozen river. She gasped for air and struggled to stay afloat, circling her arms through water so cold it burned her lungs. When at last she felt muddy ground beneath her feet, she dragged herself onto the far shore. Her clothes were soaked, and she could barely move her legs. For the final few miles, she crawled over a barren field of rocks and twigs.

"And here I am," she said with a smile.

Celia didn't know what to think. On the one hand, Slava's account of her harrowing journey gave Celia feelings of immense pride and admiration for her little sister. At the same time, the news that their family had been murdered should have created feelings of sadness and anger—but it didn't. Instead, Celia felt nothing.

Slava looked at her sister and was confused. Celia seemed to be taking the news of their family's murder so calmly that at first she wasn't sure Celia had heard her.

But Celia wasn't calm. She was numb. She had the same feeling of being numb after getting shot at in the cemetery in her hometown. It was the same feeling she had after hiding for weeks in a hole in the ground. Now her mother and sisters were dead. Once more, something horrible had happened. There was nothing Celia could say or do to make it go away. She could only marvel at how often God had disappointed her.

Celia had never been very religious, but growing up she took seriously the traditions of Judaism. As far back as she could remember, rabbis had told her, "Behave as the scripture tells us to, and God will reward you." Well, no. It seemed the world didn't work that way. At least not since Hitler came to power.

Celia reminded herself that she and her family had never asked to be born who they were. *How much suffering are we supposed to endure just for being Jews?* she wondered. Then she thought about the Nazis and another thought came to her. *What kind of person kills babies for a living? What kind of person kisses his wife and children goodbye in the morning, goes to work in a ghetto or a concentration camp, murders mothers and babies, and then comes home to have dinner with his family?*

And what kind of amazing twelve-year-old goes through what her little sister Slava went through and could still stand there smiling?

I'm not the only one who takes after our mother, Celia thought, and she embraced her sister again.

Chapter 11

PARTISANS

Celia and Slava asked Piotr what had happened to their brothers, Zalman and Hershke, and Piotr explained that he had helped their brothers join the partisans.

After Zalman and Hershke escaped from the Szarkowszczyzna ghetto, they found Piotr. He led the two brothers to a river that separated his farm from a forest on the far shore. They climbed onto a wooden raft, and Piotr paddled across the river. They climbed out on the other side, and after several hours of walking, they heard a voice calling out from behind some trees.

"Who goes there? What's the password?"

Piotr answered with the proper password, and a young partisan stepped out to greet Piotr and the two brothers. They followed the partisan through the forest and at last arrived at the campsite, where Piotr introduced them to the group leader.

"We're here to fight," Zalman said, gesturing to himself and Hershke.

"Welcome," the leader replied. "We're glad to add two strong men to our crew."

Piotr had helped the brothers reach the partisans, and now he needed the brothers' help in return. He gave Celia and Slava some bread, waited until they were back in the hole under the barn, and promised to return as soon as possible. Then he crossed the river and moved cautiously and quickly through the forest to the partisan encampment. He found the two brothers and explained the situation.

"I'm doing my best to hide your sisters," he said. "When it was just Celia, the odds were good she'd be safe. But the Nazis have increased the search for Jews. Now both your sisters are at my farm, and the danger of them being discovered is too great. At least one of them should join you here. I can keep Celia. She's older. But I recommend you let me bring Slava here to you."

"You're right about the Nazis stepping up the hunt for Jews," Zalman said. "We received the same report. Groups like ours are doing good work blowing up the Nazis' supply lines. Killing us and any other Jews in hiding has become Hitler's priority. Okay, first we need to see for ourselves if Slava is in good enough shape to live like a partisan. Then we'll make a recommendation to our group leader. If we get his permission, we'll bring her here."

That night, the brothers set out with Piotr. It was pitch-black when they crossed the river and arrived at his farm. Rain clouds thundered in the distance. Piotr brought the brothers into his barn, and all three shoveled away the sand and manure. They lifted the wooden panel. Celia and Slava climbed out and threw themselves into their brothers' arms.

Celia delivered the news that their parents, their sisters, and their sisters' children were all dead. Hershke and Zalman bowed their heads and said a quick prayer. "May their souls rest in peace—amen." There was no time for more than that.

"Slava, despite all that you've been through, you seem healthy," Zalman said. "We'll go back and make our recommendation. If it's approved, we'll come back to get you."

Hershke pulled Celia aside. He did not want Slava to hear what he had to say.

"Nazis are conducting raids all over this area," he whispered. "Chances are, they'll show up here in the next few days." He reached into his jacket pocket, pulled out a pistol, and placed it into Celia's hands.

"Take this," he said. "If the Nazis come before we return,

use it. You don't want to get caught alive." Celia had never held a pistol before. It felt dangerous and strange, but adapting to things that were dangerous and strange had become her daily life. She put the pistol in her pants pocket.

Zalman and Hershke hugged their sisters and said goodbye. They shook Piotr's hand and thanked him again for his kindness. Then they headed quickly back to the forest.

Celia and Slava climbed back into the hole. The hole had already been small when Celia was hiding in it by herself. With Slava wedged in next to her, there was barely room to breathe. Piotr covered the hole with the wooden panel. He shoveled sand and manure over the panel, then headed back to his family's farmhouse.

Within an hour, the clouds burst and rain fell like ocean waves. It filled trenches and flooded the surrounding fields. The rainwater rose and seeped into the barn. It mixed with dirt and animal manure, and the smelly slush trickled into the hole where the sisters lay squeezed together. The rain continued to fall, and soon the only parts of their bodies above water were their noses. The sisters remained under foul sludge for the next two days.

On the morning of the third day, the rain stopped. Several hours later, it began draining away. Piotr came to the barn and helped Celia and Slava climb out of the muddy hole. The sisters had a few minutes to stretch their bodies and eat the little bit of food Piotr had managed to find for them. They stank of urine and rat droppings, of sweat and dirty clothes, of manure and mud, but there was no time to wash. Their troubles were only beginning.

As Hershke had predicted, soldiers appeared in the distance marching toward Piotr's farm. Quickly, the sisters jumped back in the hole. Piotr covered it with the wood panel, shoveled hay and manure over it, and walked out to greet the soldiers.

"We're commandeering your barn," the Nazi leader told Piotr. "Bring us food."

The troops swarmed into the barn and set up a command post. Two soldiers positioned a longwave radio on a table and moved the table right over the hole where Celia and Slava lay hiding. Celia kept her hands wrapped around the pistol her brother had given her. The sisters breathed as quietly as possible and did not move a muscle.

They stayed like that for hours, not making a sound. When they had to go to the bathroom, they did so in their clothes. The soldiers over their heads ran in and out of the barn, barked orders, monitored their radio. The commotion lasted through the night.

The next morning, there was silence. Celia and Slava looked at each other, wondering what was going on above them. Then they heard three knocks on the wood panel. It was a signal from Piotr. The soldiers had left.

Piotr uncovered the hole, and the sisters climbed weakly out and collapsed, exhausted and starving, on the floor of the barn. Spending so much time in that horrible, smelly hole had become worse than torture. But they had no choice. It was either life in a hole or death at the hands of Nazis.

That night, through gaps in the wood siding of the barn, Celia and Slava watched with painful sadness as Polish farmers in horse-drawn wagons rolled by, delivering captured Jewish men, women, and children to trains for deportation to death camps and other Nazi murder sites.

THE CAMPS

Between 1933 and 1945, Nazi Germany established more than 44,000 camps of various types for the imprisonment and murder of Jews and other so-called enemies. Not all camps were concentration camps, although all camps are often mistakenly referred to in that way.

Concentration camps were specifically for the detention of civilians whom the Nazis considered "enemies of the state," such as political prisoners, Roma ("Gypsies"), Jehovah's Witnesses, homosexuals, others accused of "antisocial" behavior, and above all, Jews.

Some camps were primarily for forced labor, where prisoners were made to work twelve hours a day or more laying roads, digging ditches, or manufacturing weapons and supplies. Although labor camps were not overtly meant to kill prisoners, hundreds of thousands still died from ill-treatment, overwork, disease, and starvation.

Transit camps were temporary holding facilities for Jews

awaiting deportation to more permanent camps such as Bergen-Belsen or Auschwitz.

Prisoner-of-war camps were for captured enemies, such as American, French, Polish, and Russian soldiers. The Nazis operated nearly one thousand such camps during World War II.

Killing centers or death camps such as Treblinka were for the assembly-line murder of large numbers of people immediately upon arrival. Nearly a million people, mostly Jews, were killed just at Treblinka during the fifteen months of its operation.

Some camps changed status over time. Auschwitz, the largest of all camps, began as a detention center after Germany's invasion of Poland. By mid-1942, Jews arriving at Auschwitz were immediately gassed to death, and the camp became a death camp in its true sense.

Chapter 12

A RIVER TO NOWHERE

Early in the morning, Zalman left the partisan camp and came back to Piotr's farm.

"It's all set," he said. "Slava, you're coming with us."

Piotr turned to the two sisters. "You know I like you both," he said. "I don't want you to go. But the Germans have stepped up their search for Jews in hiding. If they find you here, they'll kill all of us. Celia is old enough that my family can pretend she is a cousin visiting for the winter. But Slava, you have to join your brothers in the forest right away. I hope that's okay with you."

"Okay?" Slava cried out. "It's the best news ever. I couldn't take living in that hole a minute longer. I'm ready now. Let's go!"

Slava kissed Celia and Piotr goodbye and set out with Zalman for the partisan camp.

When they reached the river, Zalman took his sister in his arms and waded across. The river was part of a vast watery network. Bays, rivers, and streams crisscrossed most of northern Poland. The waters fed lush, dense forests that, over hundreds of years, had grown dark and mysterious. The forests had inspired legends of frog-princesses and man-wolves, dancing demons, and handsome heroes cursed to live in the bodies of trees until true love set them free. The journey to the partisan camp took most of the day, and Zalman recited some of the fairy tales to keep his sister calm.

Meanwhile, Piotr had brought Celia from the barn to his family's house. He gave her clothes and a room to change in. "We have friends coming for dinner," he said. "If you are going to pretend to be a Christian cousin, you better start now."

Celia took a pair of scissors, trimmed her hair, washed her face, put on a dress, and practiced smiling. It had been a long time since she'd smiled. She didn't want a sad face to give her away. She gathered whatever energy she could muster after being in a hole for so long, came out of the room, and sat down at the family table with a big smile.

A few minutes later, three guests arrived. Celia looked up and inhaled sharply. She recognized one of them. Her name was Helena, a Polish Christian girl who had gone to the same school as Celia. Standing next to Helena was Helena's younger sister. The third person was a man in a uniform, clearly some kind of official who had business with Piotr's family.

The situation was serious. If Helena recognized Celia and told the official that she was a Jew, Celia would be shot. Piotr and his family would probably also be killed for hiding a Jew.

Celia watched as Helena's eyes grew big. She *did* recognize Celia. But to Celia's great relief, Helena said nothing. Celia wondered why and calculated that Helena was staying quiet to protect Piotr.

The group ate their dinner, and afterward the German official conducted his survey of the property. Then he left. Piotr pulled Celia aside.

"We can't risk that happening again," he whispered. "It was my mistake, thinking I could keep you with us. You have to join your sister and brothers—now."

He took her by the hand and brought her to the edge of the river. He pointed to the dense forest on the other side. "When you get there, just keep walking straight. The partisans will find you."

Celia climbed onto the makeshift raft that had carried her brothers across just a few weeks before. After so many months in a hole, she was exhausted and lay on the raft, staring up at the night sky.

Piotr waded into the water and gently pushed the raft, and it slowly drifted toward the other side of the river. Celia turned her head to the far shore as the raft carried her away from the only reality she had ever known. Her dreamlike former life in Szarkowszczyzna had been destroyed by a nightmare. Hitler and his Nazi thugs wanted her dead. Classmates and neighbors wanted her dead. To stay alive, she was floating on a raft that would take her to a new hiding place—or maybe she would reach the other side of the river and get shot. Nothing was certain. There was no way of predicting how long she would survive.

Why should I live, she wondered, *when so many others have been tortured and killed?*

Chapter 13

HORSES AND GUNS

The raft reached the opposite shore, and Celia climbed carefully onto dry ground. Her body was stiff, her legs felt weak as toothpicks, and she stumbled on roots and rocks. She walked as best she could through the forest. Hours passed.

From the darkness of the forest, a voice whispered, "Who goes there?"

"I'm a Jew," she said.

"What's your name?"

"Celia Cimmer."

"How do I know you are who you say?"

"My two brothers, Zalman and Hershke, and my sister Slava are with you."

From the forest emerged a group of partisans. It took Celia a moment to realize what she was seeing. These were not professional soldiers wearing crisp uniforms and shiny boots, but young people like herself, wearing old caps, soiled layers of clothing, and shoes so worn they were falling apart. These young people were lean like she was from lack of food, and their hair was matted and uncut. Around their necks hung aging rifles on frayed cloth straps. Celia noticed that they smelled bad. Then she remembered where they were. Forests didn't have showers, only swamps.

She noted something else about the partisans. They had an expression of seriousness in their eyes that made them look much older.

"Come with us," one of them said.

The partisans led Celia through the forest on a path so overgrown with weeds and vines she wondered how they could possibly know where they were going. Three hours later, as the sun rose and the air began to warm, they emerged in a clearing full of people. Living in a hole in the ground had been a lonely business. By comparison, the partisan encampment was like a bustling market, with so much going on her eyes didn't know where to focus.

Then she spotted Slava and her brothers, and the siblings fell into each other's arms. Slava, Zalman, and Hershke showed Celia around the camp. Scattered everywhere were trenches covered with branches and leaves. Each hole in the ground was carefully camouflaged to look like the forest floor. Heads poked out and watched as Celia followed her siblings around.

At least their holes look comfortable, she thought.

They arrived at the middle of the camp. One area was a munitions workshop, with rocks and tree trunks serving as tables. A handful of people were sorting bullets by size and packing them into cloth pouches. Others were cleaning the stocks of rifles with bits of rags, oiling the bolts and triggers with their fingers, and using twigs wrapped in cloth to flush gunpowder residue from the metal barrels.

Another area of the encampment was dedicated to kitchen duties. This area was staffed mostly by young women, their hair tucked up under stained headbands and a variety of hats and caps. Celia watched as a few of the women counted potatoes and sorted them into small piles on dented metal plates. Others used daggers and hunting knives to cut some kind of meat into strips. A pot of water boiled over a wood-stoked fire.

Celia looked up and saw men with guns stationed around the periphery of the camp, facing out, toward the surrounding forest. She noticed that even the people doing the sorting and cooking had rifles hanging from their shoulders. Then she remembered what Zalman had said, that Nazis were stepping up their search for partisans. Clearly, the group was ready to flee or fight at a moment's notice.

One of the women from the kitchen area walked up and handed Celia a tin plate. There wasn't much on it, a few beans, a bit of meat that might have been from a dead horse, and a potato skin.

"Some days are better than others for food," the woman said. "We raid nearby villages. Sometimes we find supplies or a few farm animals. Just as often, we go hungry."

One of the scouts who brought her to the camp pointed to the kitchen area. "Report over there," he said. "You can help skin pigs."

"That's not why I'm here," Celia said. "I'm here to fight."

The young man looked her up and down and shook his head. After months without adequate food or exercise, Celia was thin and pale.

"You're too weak to fight," he said. "Besides, what do you know about fighting? We ride fast. We shoot to kill. We boobytrap train tracks. We blow up things. Can you do any of that?"

Celia looked him in the eyes. "Try me," she said without blinking.

The scout walked over to a small group on the periphery of the camp and spoke to them in a low voice. Celia waited and tried to look more confident than she felt. The scout pointed to Celia, then exchanged nods with the men and came back.

"We'll try you out," he said.

Over the next several days, Celia learned how to be a partisan.

A young woman wearing pants stiff with dirt and a shirt three sizes too big was given the duty of showing Celia how to care for a horse. There were at least thirty horses grazing around the camp. The horses were short and stocky, mostly mousy gray and dirty brown, their coats so dull they practically blended with the surrounding trees and bushes. Celia was surprised that despite their small size, the horses looked very strong.

"They're Konik horses," the young woman said. "Not so pretty, but good workers, and they don't need any special food. They eat grass, roots, shrubs, whatever they can find. They store a lot of fat. Thick skin, too, so they stay warm in cold weather."

The young woman walked over to one of the horses and patted it on the head. "This one will be yours," she said.

When she was a young girl, Celia's father had allowed her to ride the workhorses that he used to transport bolts of flax from his factory to customers. Celia was good at riding and knew how to approach a horse. She walked up to the one that would be hers, staying steady and calm, without fear or uncertainty, showing the horse she was in charge without being aggressive. She laid a reassuring hand on the horse's withers, the part of his back between his shoulder blades, and stroked him gently. She took the horse's head between her two hands and looked him in the eyes. They stayed like that for a few moments, locked in a silent gaze.

The young woman charged with training her was impressed.

Another partisan took charge of showing Celia how to load and shoot a gun. Even to Celia, who knew very little about guns, the meager supply of weapons looked insufficient. Most of the guns were worn and scratched rifles and pistols, rusty and tarnished with age. Hardly any of the guns were new. Most appeared to be leftovers from the First World War, about thirty years before. Other guns looked like they had been assembled from various parts captured during raids. Some of the barrels needed straightening and could not be counted on to fire when needed. Repairs and test-firing went on every day.

Soon Celia became as good at shooting as she was at riding. After several days, the group leader walked up to her. "We have some missions coming up," he said. "Keep training. Maybe you can come with us."

Daring, Celia told herself. *Just like Mama.*

Chapter 14

TO LIVE OR DIE IN THE FOREST

Celia was impressed by how much her brothers were respected by the other partisans. This was a Russian unit, and there were few Jews. Nonetheless, the two brothers had quickly adapted to life in the forest and had become leaders of the group. Zalman in particular was dedicated to bringing down as many Nazis as possible.

Celia was even more impressed at seeing how well Slava had adapted to partisan life. At twelve, Slava was too young for combat, but she took as much risk as anyone in handling other responsibilities. On days when there were no missions, Slava helped keep the encampment running smoothly. She set out alone into the surrounding woods to bring back supplies of wood. She stoked the campfires, hauled pails of water, and kept watch at night. In just a short time, Slava proved herself equal to any of the older partisans.

In battle, if the partisans were fired on, it was Slava who crawled across the ground to where the wounded had fallen. She untied the rope she used to hold up her pants, looped the rope around their bodies, and crawled back with the rope in her teeth. She handed the rope to others, and they dragged their comrades to safety.

Mornings were the busiest time for Slava and the other women partisans, who had at most two hours to build a fire and cook food for the entire camp. For all partisans, the rest of the day was filled with organizing raids, setting up and repairing the camp, doing laundry, cleaning weapons, and caring for the wounded. At the end of each day, before sunset, Slava extinguished the campfires so that no smoke drifted up to give away their position.

Some of the women partisans worked undercover. They dressed in civilian clothes, walked out of the forest, and blended with the general population in surrounding towns, where they secured supplies, delivered messages to contacts, and gathered information.

Celia and Slava learned their combat lessons well. They mastered the technique of making Molotov cocktails by filling bottles with gasoline and inserting a cloth fuse. They learned where to position dynamite under trains and trucks and when to detonate an explosion for greatest impact. Sabotaging transports was particularly important, as Nazi forces across Europe received the bulk of their ammunition, food, medicine, and other necessities by truck and by train.

A priority for partisans was disrupting the flow of these supplies by any means possible. The partisans blew up railway ties and bridges. They toppled trees to block roads. When trucks loaded with supplies were forced to stop, the partisans descended on them, held up the drivers at gunpoint, and made off with whatever supplies they could carry.

The partisans hid by day and traveled and fought by night. They lived off the land, slept in makeshift dugouts, and looked after one another. Celia and Slava dug their own trenches and covered them with branches and leaves. Freezing temperatures, lack of warm clothing, scarcity of food, and the constant dangers of frostbite and disease affected all partisans. Staying alive was a full-time job.

Under no circumstances would partisans allow themselves to be captured. Whenever Celia and Slava left the camp, they carried two grenades. One for the Nazis and one for themselves. They refused to be taken alive.

RESISTANCE

Resistance is a term that, in the context of the Holocaust, most often refers to fighting back with weapons against the Nazis. But there were other forms of resistance as well. The Nazis outlawed the Jewish religion, and Jews who nonetheless continued to hold religious services were performing a kind of resistance. Nazi law forbade Jewish children from attending school, and so holding classes in secret was also a kind of resistance. Other forms of resistance included staging artistic performances, listening to underground news reports on radios, and aiding Jews in escaping Nazi persecution. All these acts were illegal under Nazi law, and defying any Nazi law constituted an act of resistance.

Organized armed combat was the most forceful form of Jewish resistance, and partisan fighting groups existed across Nazi-occupied Europe. Partisans knew that their resistance activities would not stop the Germans. Still, they fought, even under the most adverse conditions.

Chapter 15

THE NIGHT BEFORE

At dinnertime, Celia stood in line, holding her dented tin plate and cup. A young woman dipped a metal ladle into a steaming pot of beans and potato skins and served her a small portion. Celia sat with Slava, Hershke, and Zalman. While she ate, she glanced around the encampment and studied the faces of her comrades. Just a few years before, they might have been climbing trees or doing homework. Now they were blowing up trains and shooting Nazis.

Like her, these partisans had lost family, friends, and homes. A few had managed to escape from concentration camps. The stories they told haunted Celia and would not go away. One escapee from a camp started to tell his story, then paused, half-hypnotized by his own memories, then came back a moment later as if waking up from a dream. He described things the Nazis did to prisoners that served no purpose other than to cause excruciating pain. Celia had to walk away. Hearing such things was itself a kind of torture.

Like Celia, the people around her became partisans not because they were natural-born fighters. They became partisans because they wanted revenge for what the Nazis had done to their homeland, their families, and other innocent people. Without having to say it out loud, Celia knew each of them was thinking the same thing: *If we're going to die anyway, let's bring down a few bad guys first.*

At night, if they were sure no one could see the flames, Celia and her comrades built a campfire. They sat around the fire and shared memories and talked about what life would be like when the war was finally over. One of the partisans had no patience for such dreaming and commented, "I just want to fight the Nazis." Then they went silent, each one lost in their own thoughts, remembering loved ones murdered or deported and never heard from again.

After dark, if there was no wind and their voices might be heard in the silence, they sat without speaking, and the only sounds were the crackling of the fire and the croaking of frogs in nearby swamps. If a wolf or raccoon wandered by and happened to snap a twig, the group slowly reached for their rifles, on guard against a sneak attack.

On nights when there was enough wind to muffle their voices, they sat huddled together around the campfire and quietly sang the hymn of Jewish partisans. The song had been written in 1943 by Hirsh Glik, a young prisoner of the Vilna ghetto, and it quickly became the anthem of resistance against Nazi persecution. No partisan, Jew or non-Jew, could remain indifferent to its lyrics, as the words came from a place deep in the heart where survival itself was the ultimate act of resistance.

Never say this road is the final one for you,
Though a leaden sky covers over days of blue.
As the fateful hour awaiting us all comes near,
Our marching steps proclaim the message
—"We are here!"

. . . Tomorrow's sun will surely brighten our day,
And our foes with yesterday will fade away.
But if the sun delays, and far away must remain,
This warm song, our hymn, the generations will maintain.

This song, written with blood and not pencil lead,
Is hardly the kind of tune birds sing overhead.
It is a hymn sung by people under a collapsing wall.
With grenades in hand, they heed its call.

Therefore, never say this road is the final one for you,

Though a leaden sky covers over days of blue.

As the fateful hour awaiting us comes near,

Our marching steps proclaim the message

—"We are here!"

Chapter 16

MISSION IMPOSSIBLE

Nighttime. The only sounds were the clicking of crickets and the rustling of leaves on the trees. Thirty partisans were saddled and ready to ride. Celia saw her comrades looking up at the night sky, calculating whether the moon was too bright. A clear moonlit sky meant being easily seen, and the mission would have to be postponed. Clouds or rain made for better cover.

The sky was cloudy. The mission was on.

Celia cinched the strap of her rifle across her chest and tightened her grip on the horse's reins, preparing for a tough ride.

The day before, a scout had returned from reconnaissance in a nearby town. He reported that Nazi soldiers had built an ammunition dump on the grounds of an old school. The partisans needed weapons, but they also needed to disarm their enemy. Blowing up the ammunition dump would be as good as securing the weapons for themselves.

The leader signaled with a wave of his hand, and the

partisans set out, riding their horses as silently as the forest underbrush allowed.

A few hours later, they spotted the target. In the middle of a schoolyard, silhouetted against the starlit sky, were boxes of dynamite, barrels of gunpowder, belts of bullets, and other weapons stacked up in a tall pile. At the far end of the yard stood an abandoned schoolhouse. Celia could hear German voices coming from inside—men talking and laughing.

The partisans didn't have much time to do their job.

Silently, they led their horses into the yard. Celia and the other teenage girl took up positions at the far end of the yard and kept their rifles pointed toward the schoolhouse. Several young men jumped off their horses, lit gasoline-soaked rags, threw them onto the pile of ammunition, jumped back on their horses, and rode off at a gallop. Celia and the other girl followed close behind.

Seconds later, the pile of ammunition exploded with a deafening roar. The air smelled of burning gunpowder, and bullets popped like strings of firecrackers. Celia's horse reared up on his hind legs. Celia's rifle got tangled in the reins, and she fell to the ground. Her horse galloped off. Nazi soldiers burst from the schoolhouse, yelling and firing their weapons into the darkness.

Two soldiers lit flares and tossed them forward. The schoolyard burst into light. Celia was lying on the ground, exposed and alone. No gun. No horse.

The soldiers took aim.

In the distance, one of the partisans turned his horse around and saw Celia stranded on the ground. He galloped back into the yard. The flares faded, and the soldiers shot into the darkness, missing their targets. The partisan reached down, grabbed Celia's hand, pulled her up and onto his saddle, then galloped off to rejoin the other partisans.

The munitions pile exploded a second time. Celia and her comrade looked back and saw Nazi bodies scattered across the schoolyard.

On this raid, the partisans lost no one. The numbers at the end of other raids were not always so good.

Chapter 17

BACK TO LIFE

The partisan who had saved Celia's life had known her for less than a month. In that sense, he was a stranger. So were the other fifty or so people on whom her life now depended—people who, in any other world, might never have known one another. In any other world, they may have had nothing in common. But here, in their shared world of hunger and death camps, they were closer than friends. A firm and fast bond held them together in this time of catastrophe. Social differences fell away, political differences became irrelevant, and human frailties were more easily forgiven. Cooperation in the fight against Nazis was their common cause. They had become extensions of one another, one person in fifty bodies, synchronized in staying alive.

The next day, Celia watched her brothers, Zalman and Hershke, navigate through the encampment, discussing missions with other partisan leaders and planning next moves, and again she felt proud seeing how much the others respected her brothers.

Slava, on the other hand, had Celia worried. Slava was smaller, younger, and in Celia's opinion, not cut out for partisan life. *She's smart and should be in school*, Celia thought, *not scavenging in a forest and blowing things up.*

A few days later, the partisans conducted another raid. This time, they captured a young German soldier who had been wounded and was unable to flee. The partisan leader knew what the Germans had done to Celia's family and shoved the young captive in her direction.

"He's all yours," the leader said. "Do whatever you want."

Celia pointed her rifle at the soldier. Like her sister, he was very young. She noted that he wore the uniform of an adult but had the face of a boy. If he traded his uniform for baggy pants and a sweater, he'd look like one of the partisans. The boy stared at her. Celia smelled a dank odor coming from his clothes, part sweat, part fear. She hadn't expected to feel compassion for someone who wanted her dead. She put her gun down, bandaged his knee, and brought him a plate of food.

Some of the other partisans watched her with contempt. It didn't matter to them how young the boy was. Celia was caring for a Nazi soldier who had tried to kill them. No one had forced him to be a Nazi. The Jews were being hunted by many Nazis who were just as young as this one. Should they all be forgiven? This wasn't the time for soft hearts. It was the time to kill or be killed. Most of the partisans felt that way.

A few had a different point of view. They knew that the teenagers who volunteered to become Hitler Youth were not born hating Jews. They'd learned to hate Jews from their parents and neighbors, from the government, from newspapers, from radio propaganda, and from their teachers. In high school during the Nazi era, German students attended vile classes called raciology—Rassenkunde—that were required by the government.

The course proposed that Jews were not human beings. They were like bacteria that had to be eliminated. The course was based on made-up science and fake biological and genetic arguments. It was created from ignorance and cruelty, and it was taught by hateful people. No doubt the young soldier at Celia's mercy had taken the course. It may have formed his understanding of reality. It may have even been his reason for becoming a soldier and wanting to kill Jews—that, and the fact that if he refused, his superiors in the Hitler Youth would have sent him to a concentration camp for disobeying orders.

To Jew-hating Germans, a boy-soldier like this one was a

hero. To the partisans, he was a murderer. To Celia, he was a child who had been born on the wrong side of history, like her classmate who'd decided they weren't best friends anymore because Celia was a Jew. *People like them may be victims of Nazi propaganda, but they aren't fit to shine the shoes of someone like Piotr,* she thought to herself.

She wondered if she was being more generous than she should be, but by thinking of Piotr and the compassion he'd shown her, she came down on the side of cleaning the German boy's wounds and feeding him a plate of food.

The next morning, she didn't see the young soldier. During the night, the partisans had marched him off somewhere. She didn't ask what they'd done to him.

Summer 1944 arrived. The war was going badly for the Germans. Celia's unit had begun receiving supplies air-dropped by Soviet planes. The partisans now had a longwave radio and could hear reports about movements of the Nazi army. They knew about victories by the Americans and British in the western part of Europe and by the Soviets to the east. The good guys were making steady progress, liberating cities and towns that had been under Nazi occupation for years.

The liberation of Poland from Nazi occupation didn't happen all at once. It took place over the course of a year, but eventually, by the end of 1944, the war was over for the people of Poland.

But not for Celia, Slava, or their two brothers. They were alone, with no home to go back to. The world they had grown up in—their beautiful family house on the market square, Sunday movies projected onto a big white sheet, holiday dinners with family, the world where people were rewarded for doing good, where things made sense—that world was dead. The Nazis had killed it.

Memories of what they'd suffered, on the other hand, remained very much alive. The rest of the world was celebrating the end of the war. For survivors such as Celia and her siblings, the hard times were far from over.

Chapter 18

LIVING MEMORY

Celia felt almost no joy when the war ended. Yes, she was glad the Nazis had finally been defeated. Yes, she was glad that Slava and their two brothers had survived. But their parents had been murdered along with the rest of their family, their friends had been killed, their home had been destroyed, and she had witnessed horrors no human being should be made to see. Happiness no longer had a place in her world. Her memories were dark, the future grim, and she suffered from loneliness even more than during the war years.

Why? Because so long as she was in the ghetto, so long as she was in a hole under Piotr's barn, or so long as she was a partisan, Celia was preoccupied with staying alive. After liberation, she no longer had survival to keep her distracted. After liberation, she was alone with her memories, and they were too hard to bear. Insomnia became a way of life. She dared not go to sleep. The nightmares were too real.

Soviet army officers gave Celia and her siblings a room

where they could live for a while. The room was tiny, but compared to a hole in the ground with rats, it was like paradise. For the moment, Celia and her siblings could rest, think, and consider what to do with their lives.

Slava knew what she wanted to do. She wanted to become a midwife and help pregnant women. She found work in a refugee hospital. Two years later, she received her nursing degree.

Hershke and Zalman knew what they wanted to do. They wanted to live in Israel. They made their way to Jerusalem, where they found work, married, and started families of their own.

Celia had no idea what she wanted to do, and she was too tired to care. She felt no emotions, not even hatred for her Nazi tormentors. Something was broken inside her. She loved her siblings but could not express her love. She was indifferent to everything.

"I was alive," she later said of this time, "but that was all."

Celia had wanted a life like other girls her age. But when other girls were holding the hands of their boyfriends, Celia was holding the trigger of a rifle. For the so-called "crime" of being a Jew, she had been beaten, starved, left for dead, and exposed to the worst in human nature. Her faith in people was crushed, her hopes for the future gone. She felt nothing.

"Alive, but that was all."

Soon after the end of the war, Celia met a young Jewish man named Kopl Kossovski. Within three weeks of their first meeting, Kopl turned to Celia and asked, "Do you want to marry me?"

"Why not?" Celia said.

They married in 1944. There was no courtship, no romance or fireworks. They barely knew each other. Kopl was a decent person, he understood what Jews had been through, and he was available. What more did she need? Love? Dreams? Those were for other people.

In 1945, Celia gave birth to a son. She and Kopl named him Samuel, after Celia's father, Shmuel. Celia had mixed feelings about bringing a child into a world that had created Nazis and ghettos and concentration camps. For a long time, she was unable to care for her son, and Sam spent his early life in the care of his uncle Zalman and his wife, Sonia.

In 1949, Celia took back custody of her son, and she, Kopl, and Sam immigrated to the United States, where they settled in New Haven, Connecticut. Kopl changed the family's last name to Kassow, figuring it would be easier for Americans to pronounce.

Celia and Kopl had two more children, daughters whom

they named Linda and Cheryl after Celia's mother and aunt. Kopl became a tailor and Celia worked odd jobs, including as a waitress and driving instructor. She also helped émigrés get the assistance they needed to build a new life in America. She didn't tell her children about what she had gone through during the war. Why expose them to such tragedy?

However, when Sam entered college, he had a girlfriend who was not Jewish, and Celia openly expressed reservations about the relationship.

"My mother told me that, because of what happened to us as Jews, I should not marry a non-Jewish woman," Sam later told an interviewer. "She hinted that she had given something up, and that caused her a lot of pain, and I would have to give something up, too. I didn't know what she meant until I was in my forties.

"That's when I learned that Piotr, the young Polish farmer who had saved my mother and her sister, had been in love with her," Sam explained. "Piotr risked his life by rescuing her from the Glubok ghetto and hiding her in his barn. My mother didn't say it, but she hinted that she felt terribly guilty that she did not marry him. I think she never got over that."

Celia's husband, Kopl, was a wonderful, hardworking man and a caring and loving father. He and Celia built a good home for their children. Celia's son, Sam Kassow, became a renowned Holocaust scholar. In addition to writing acclaimed books and giving popular lectures, he curated museum exhibits and produced documentary films.

Sam's career frequently took him to Poland. On one of these trips, he brought along his family, including his aunt Slava; his sisters, Linda and Cheryl; and Slava's children Deena and Steve. They all went looking for Piotr, and they found him living on the same farm where he and his parents had lived when he was a boy.

Piotr was now in his seventies, married, and a father. When Piotr saw Slava, the first thing he said was, "Hello, Squirt!" Slava had been scared that sad memories might come back from seeing Piotr, but with his happy, playful greeting, Piotr erased all her anxieties. The reunion was a happy one, tearful and heartfelt.

Celia and Piotr, however, never met again.

Chapter 19

THE WORLD SHOULD NEVER FORGET

The Holocaust—the systematic, state-sponsored murder of European Jews—was the result of hatred, corruption, ignorance, cruelty, and ultimately indifference toward the fate of Jews. People had been taught to distrust Jews, to despise them, to want them killed. Nazi propaganda was so effective at preying on that distrust of Jews that even killing Jews was not enough. People wanted to see them humiliated and tortured as well. Celia did not want to relive those horrible years, but she felt it was her duty to describe what she had gone through. Future generations needed to know, and only those who had survived the Holocaust could describe it from personal experience. At age fifty-six, Celia—now known by her married name, Celia Kassow—agreed to record her experiences for the Fortunoff Video Archive for Holocaust Testimonies at Yale University.

She arrived at the recording studio in New Haven, Connecticut, in February 1980. Her hearing, which had been almost completely destroyed by soldiers' bullets forty years before, had never fully returned, and from time to time, she had to ask the interviewer to repeat a question.

When you watch the video, you become aware of something else that never went away. It's something Celia communicates with her eyes. They are the eyes of someone who has seen how low human beings can fall when they turn away from their better nature. They are also the eyes of someone who has seen how high human beings can soar when they keep the flame of that better nature burning bright—people like Piotr, who risked his life to save Jews. People like Celia's siblings, who fought with the partisans in the woods. People like Celia's parents, who did all they could, until the end, to protect their family.

The recording took a full day. When Celia's family drove her home that evening, the sun was setting over New Haven. It had rained that afternoon, and lightning pulsed now and then in the distance. The windows were closed against the cold February wind, but the car was warm with the closeness of her family.

Perhaps Celia slept better that night, having at last

unburdened herself from dark memories of a time when she had been a fighter in the woods. A time when she and a handful of other young people had decided together that, rather than just be killed, they preferred to go down fighting.

Author's Note

Real-life stories of young people who resisted Nazi tyranny during World War II convey the importance of taking initiative and persevering despite impossible odds. At the same time, Holocaust educators caution us to not glamorize their achievements or exaggerate their motives. Young partisans fought Nazis not because they were fearless heroes. They fought because they expected to die and preferred to bring down a few Nazis first.

Some resisters such as Celia managed to escape death by the thinnest of odds. Her story reads like an adventure tale, but she did not have superhuman powers, nor did she possess any unique will to survive. Like many other young women who joined the partisans, Celia considered herself an ordinary person. She and her comrades only became extraordinary when they were tested under extraordinary circumstances.

Telling Celia's story was challenging for many reasons. The writing, for instance, had to be accurate, since inaccuracies are seized upon by those who deny the Holocaust ever happened.

"There, you see?" deniers say. "That detail is historically wrong, so the whole thing must be invented." Complete accuracy, however, is not always possible. To give one example, in her testimony, Celia describes returning home from school in June 1941 and finding her house inside the fence of a ghetto. Historically, the ghetto in her town did not officially open until October. The most likely explanation is that Celia was describing her home having been taken over by Nazi forces, even though the ghetto itself had not yet been formally established.

Still, a story has to be more than just accurate. It must also engage its readers. If it's not interesting, no one will want to read it. Occasionally, that meant taking liberties in telling Celia's story. Let me give you another example. In this book, I have quoted several conversations. The conversations *did* take place. They were mentioned in interviews given by Celia, Slava, and others who were there, but I had no audio recordings of the conservations to go by. So I created dialogue based on what I knew of those conversations.

Here's another example. There is evidence that Celia and Slava were in different partisan groups. They likely did visit each other, so the chapters you read here make sense. But in my telling, it seems as though they were in the same partisan group. That was a choice I made in order to make their story easier to follow.

For their help in keeping this biography as accurate as possible, I'm grateful to Celia's son, Sam Kassow; his sisters, Linda Astmann and Cheryl Kassow; and Slava's children, Deena Leonard and Dan and Steve Fintel. For her detailed review of the manuscript, my thanks go to Joanne Rudof of the Fortunoff Video Archive for Holocaust Testimonies. Others, including Fortunoff Archive director Stephen Naron and scholars Michael Berenbaum and the late Lawrence Langer, offered their comments and encouragement. To them as well, I extend my thanks.

For reading the manuscript to assure historical accuracy, I am thankful to the distinguished Holocaust author and educator Christoph Dieckmann.

Last but not least, I offer heartfelt thanks to my editor, Aimee Friedman, who has mastered the alchemical art of spinning literary straw into readable gold.

A person's life is complex, and a biographer has the awkward job of deciding what to include and what to leave out. Celia's youngest sister, Slava, for example, has a story just as amazing as her sister Celia's. Slava deserves a book of her own.

Here is a story about one of the brothers that I left out. At one point, while serving as a partisan, Celia was separated from her brothers. Years later, she found out Nazi soldiers had shot her older brother Hershke in the leg and he couldn't walk. He begged the other partisans to kill him rather than leave him to be found and tortured. Instead, the partisans collected a piece of gold, a watch, and any other valuables they could find and bribed a pilot to fly Hershke to safety. The plane was too small for Hershke to sit inside, so the pilot took lengths of heavy rope, strapped him to a wing of the plane, and flew him to safety.

Now, that's an amazing story, but who was this pilot? How did the partisans know to contact him? Why did the pilot agree? There were too few details, so I left this story out. By the way, we do know that Hershke survived his escape on the wing of the plane, and after the war he settled in Israel.

I would have also liked to tell more of Piotr's story. After the war, when his neighbors found out he had hidden Jews, they turned their backs on him. The Jew-haters may have lost the war but not their hatred of Jews or their disdain for those like Piotr who helped them. Piotr deserves to be recognized for saving so many lives, including those of Celia and her siblings.

How did a demagogue like Hitler succeed in turning so many people against the Jews? He did it by preying on people's fears, prejudices, bitterness, and hatred. The term sometimes used is "weaponizing" people. The Holocaust unleashed something very dark in human nature, something so cruel that even eighty years later we still haven't fully understood how it happened or what it tells us about ourselves.

I've asked many survivors what they think people should understand about the Holocaust. Here are some of the answers they gave me.

- People should know that Jews were not passive, faceless victims. They were individual men, women, and children who led meaningful lives. Many took great risks to resist the Nazi terror and fight back. Celia resisted, among other ways, by not allowing people to treat her as inferior. She refused, for example, to give in to a Nazi police chief at the risk of being shot. She also refused to let the partisans sideline her to working in a kitchen when she was quite prepared to fight.
- Non-Jews should not think the Holocaust doesn't concern them. Hatred of anyone concerns all of us, and we need to be alert to its symptoms. It can begin with something as small as name-calling and end in mass murder.
- Resistance did not mean only shooting a gun. Resistance also meant defying Nazi orders, for example by recording events

in secret diaries and preserving Jewish culture by holding classes and religious services that were forbidden by Nazi law.

- Young people are never irrelevant. Throughout history, young people motivated by noble intentions have made dramatic improvements to a problematic world.

Most of all, survivors I spoke with wanted readers to know that the Holocaust must never be forgotten and that an important way of remembering is through the testimonies of eyewitnesses who were there—eyewitnesses such as Celia Kassow.

Joshua M. Greene

2024

Turn the page to see photographs of Celia, Slava, other partisan fighters, and more.

Celia Kassow.

Celia's sister, Slava.

Jewish people working in a shoe factory in the Szarkowszczyzna ghetto.

Jewish children making boxes in the Glubok ghetto.

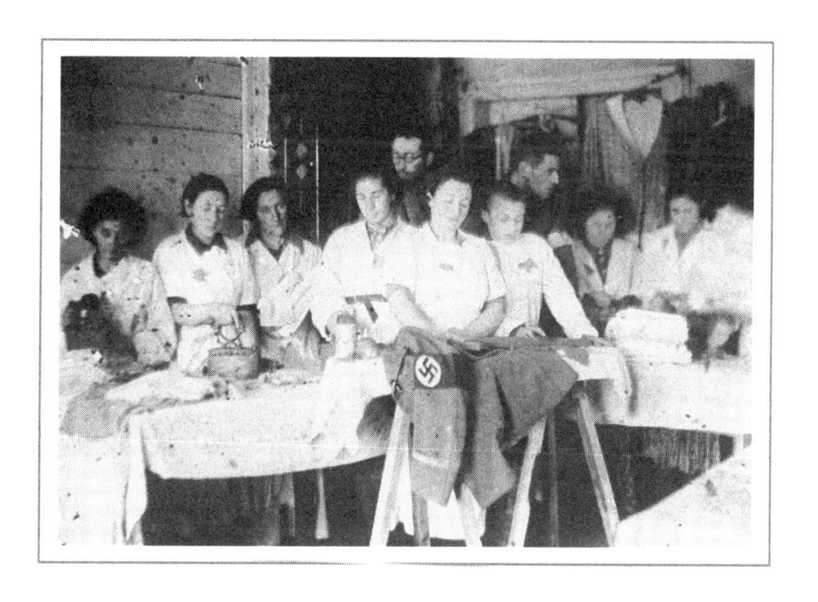

A group of Jewish women press Nazi military uniforms in the Glubok ghetto.

A group of Jewish partisans during the war.

A group of partisans on guard duty.

Slava (front row, far left) with members
of her partisan brigade.

Celia with her husband and son after the war.

Photo Credits

Photos ©: 129, 130, 136, 137: Samuel Kassow. All other photos © United States Holocaust Memorial Museum.

About the Author

Joshua M. Greene is an award-winning documentary filmmaker and the author of several acclaimed books, including *The Girl Who Fought Back: Vladka Meed and the Warsaw Ghetto Uprising*, *Signs of Survival: A Memoir of the Holocaust*, cowritten with Renee Hartman, and *My Survival: A Girl on Schindler's List*, cowritten with Rena Finder. A former instructor of Holocaust history at Hofstra and Fordham Universities, Joshua Greene sits on the Board of Advisors to the Fortunoff Video Archive for Holocaust Testimonials at Yale University. He lives in Old Westbury, New York.

TURN THE PAGE TO LEARN ABOUT
OTHER POWERFUL TRUE STORIES
OF THE HOLOCAUST.

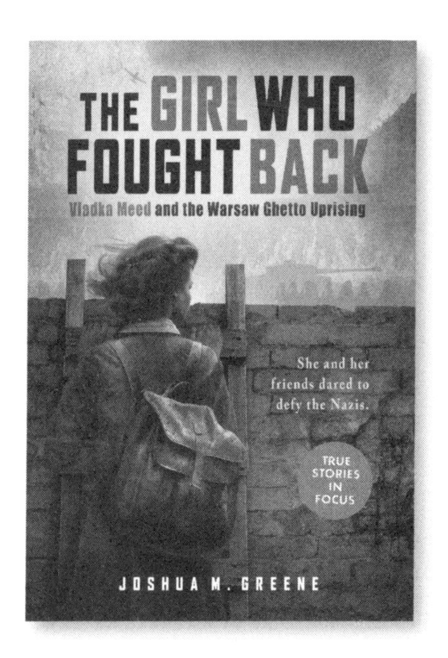

Warsaw, Poland, 1940s: The Nazis are on the march, determined to wipe out the Jewish people of Europe. Teenage Vladka and her family are among the thousands of Jews forced to relocate behind the walls of the Warsaw Ghetto. Vladka joins up with other young people in the ghetto to resist and fight back against the Nazis, no matter the cost.

This is the astonishing true story of the Warsaw Ghetto Uprising, told through the lens of Holocaust survivor and educator Vladka Meed.

RENEE: *I was ten years old then, and my sister was eight. The responsibility was on me to warn everyone when the soldiers were coming because my sister and both my parents were deaf.*

I was my family's ears.

As Jews living in 1940s Czechoslovakia, Renee, Herta, and their parents were in immediate danger when the Holocaust came to their door. Their parents were taken away, and the two sisters went on the run. Eventually, they, too, were captured and taken to the concentration camp Bergen-Belsen. Communicating in sign language and relying on each other for strength in the midst of illness, death, and starvation, Renee and Herta would have to fight to survive the darkest of times.

Rena Finder was eleven when the Nazis forced her and her family—along with all the other Jewish people of Krakow, Poland—into the ghetto. Then Rena and her mother ended up working for Oskar Schindler, a German businessman who employed Jewish prisoners in his factory. But Rena's nightmares were not over. She and her mother were deported to the concentration camp Auschwitz. With great cunning, it was Schindler who set out to help them escape.

Ruth Gruener was a hidden child during the Holocaust. At the end of the war, she and her parents were overjoyed to be free. But their struggles as displaced people had just begun.

In war-ravaged Europe, they waited for paperwork that would grant them a chance to come to America. Once they arrived in Brooklyn, Ruth started at a new school and tried to make friends—but she continued to fight nightmares and flashbacks of her time during World War II.

The family's perseverance is a classic story of the American dream, but it also illustrates the difficulties that millions of immigrants face in the aftermath of trauma.